George Augustus Sala

After breakfast;

Or, Pictures done with a quill

George Augustus Sala

After breakfast;
Or, Pictures done with a quill

ISBN/EAN: 9783337730420

Printed in Europe, USA, Canada, Australia, Japan

Cover: Foto ©Andreas Hilbeck / pixelio.de

More available books at **www.hansebooks.com**

AFTER BREAKFAST;

OR,

PICTURES DONE WITH A QUILL.

BY

GEORGE AUGUSTUS SALA.

IN TWO VOLUMES.

VOL. II.

LONDON:

TINSLEY BROTHERS, 18, CATHERINE ST., STRAND.

1864.

CONTENTS OF VOLUME II.

AFTER BREAKFAST.

THE BLEEDING DIAMOND.

—◆—

THERE are not many things more terrible and loathsome to the traveller by steam-boat who is not thoroughly accustomed to the sad sea waves, and who has "found his sea-legs," as the phrase goes, merely to have them perpetually sliding away from under him, than the dinners provided by the principal steam-navigation companies of Europe. Dinner on board an American or West India mail-packet, or of one of the P. and O.'s magnificent vessels, is of course quite another kind of thing. You have gone through your apprenticeship of sea-sickness, and entered upon

good sound journey-work of substantial eating.
With plenty of champagne, and all the luxuries
that are out of season, with pretty ladies to talk
to, and a commander who is a gentleman to help
the soup, you enjoy your repast, and feel quite
ready for a little music or limited loo afterwards.
But, oh, those dreadful steam-boat dinners when
the voyage is as short as it is tempestuous? How
willingly would you forfeit thrice the amount of
the passage-money you have paid, adding a handsome bonus to it, to be spared the unearthly
sound of the dinner-bell, the sickening spectacle
of the steward's assistants issuing from the galley
with those appalling dishes reeking with an odour
far worse to you than bilge-water, and with their
battered pewter covers distilling drops of unc-
tuous transpiration. Boiled mutton again! Yes,
the old, old boiled mutton, with the steaming
festoons of woolly fat, the frightful yawning inci-
sion in the centre, revealing the red, red raw
within, the coagulated lumps of flour and grease,
with the small-shot dipped in verdigris and pass-

ing muster for capers, ironically served as sauce. There is that about the foggy potatoes, the misty dabs of greens, the tarts, apparently containing "*zostera marina*" stewed in molasses, the bilious cheese, and the stringy celery of a steam-boat dinner, to me inexpressibly hideous and revolting. A momentary contemplation, to say nothing of the consumption of them, will convince the strongest of humanity that he resembles a late Prince of Denmark, in having "that within which passeth show." What though the banquets—say on board the Antwerp or the Scotch boats—do consist of something else besides boiled mutton, and under ordinary circumstances would be palatable, nay, sumptuous? Of what avail are succulent cockaleekie and tender rumpsteaks to him who is afflicted with inveterate nausea? But the less said on these horrifying short sea trips the better. The theme is inexhaustible, and its bare mention reminds me of certain abominations in the way of oil, garlic, and grated cheese, in the boats of the Messageries Impériales plying between Marseilles and Genoa—but no more.

After rain should come sunshine. Let me evoke a few sunny memories of a steam-boat dinner on smooth water which can be really and thoroughly enjoyed. This is the deck of the Gross Herzog von Schweinhundhausen, Rhine steamer. It is just five o'clock, and we are sitting down to dinner. The collation takes place under a marquee extending from abaft the funnel to the stern; and the man at the wheel, visible through the opening of the tent, looks like a fresh-water toast-master. The sides, also, have apertures, revealing, as we steam along, the perpetually shifting panorama of the glorious Rhine river. The only thing conspiring to damp the felicity of the tourist in search of the picturesque is the impossibility of having eyes at the back of his head. For, while you are gloating over the beauties of the right bank, the charming features of the left have passed away. It is all very well saying that you will make up for the omission when you come back, but how do you know that you will ever return? Some cunning men have essayed to avert the deprivation by sitting on a camp-stool amidships, and doing their best, by an artful process of squinting, to take in both banks simultaneously; but I should advise you to run the risk of no such trifling with the optic nerve, and, if you are too scrupulous to commit your Murray's Guide-book well to memory, and assume on your arrival in England that you are perfectly well acquainted with everything that is to be seen on either littoral of the historic stream, the best thing you can do is to say nothing whatever about it, and allow the Rhine (which never did you any harm) to roll on in peace.

Five years since, if my memory be not playing the traitor, I was dining cheerfully, comfortably, and copiously, on board the Gross Herzog von Schweinhundhausen. Ye stewed eels, I have nothing but what is good to say of you! Ye speckled Rhine trout, ye lay not heavy in my epigastric region! Others of the fresh-water fish may have been slightly bony, remotely suggestive in their flavour of some Erd Geist, or spirit of mud, that hovered over them in their infancy; but ah! what a glorious pair of capons graced the board! What a delicious loin of veal (with plum sauce) was handed round, dissected in a manner quite foreign to our notions of culinary anatomy. And the good, honest, innocent little Rhine wines! The pale slender flasks that cheer and do not inebriate, but whose contents if you do really exceed—and there are artful Marco-brunners which are not to be resisted— will in their strong acidity leave you the next morning without any skin on your lips. And, to sum up: the dessert, the grapes, the peaches, the nectarines, the apples, and pears! It was the twenty-fourth of August; the weather was superb, and I had not yet exhausted that stock of cigars which every prudent traveller in Vater-land should be careful to bring with him from England. When dinner was over, I as carefully sat to leeward of the gentlemen who were indulging in tobacco, rolled or twisted; for the other way nausea lies, and between complacent digestion and the exquisite scenery, and the strains of a brass band which didn't play too noisily, and a popular novel—I think it was Evelina, from Herr Tauchnitz's collection—I felt myself from head to foot a lotos-eater, and wished I could eat lotoses for ever.

"The Badischer Hof at Mayence: you will stop there. It is at the Renown for Great British Travellers," the man in the sky-blue trousers observed. He had observed a great many things before. Indeed, he had been talking to me all day, and I had less listened to, than borne with him, in a kind of dreamy listlessness. His bald chat was as the babbling of a little brook which you cannot be angry with, for it suggests coolness and refreshment in the hot summer-time. As this was, however, about the twentieth time that the man in the sky-blue trousers had sung the praises of the establishment at Mayence, in whose interest I presumed him retained, I felt bound to take some notice of it and him, and said, mildly :

"Bother the Badischer Hof. I think I shall go ashore at Coblentz."

He was not one whit disconcerted. "At Coblentz? Good. You will stop, then, at the Great Black Horse. Your compatriot, the Duke of Derbyshire, always stayed there."

"Confound the Duke of Derbyshire," I murmured. "I've changed my mind, and shall land at Eisenach."

"Aha! Yes. Good," the imperturbable man in the sky-blue trousers resumed. "In that case you will descend at the Two Emperors of Siam— the well-known English aristocratic hotel. 'Tis the only place between Biberich and Bonn where you can get real Johannisburger, and Prince Metternich comes there twice a year to see that the stock has not deteriorated."

"Now look here," I broke in, quite good humouredly, but firmly. "It's no use. I mean to stop at the hotel—wherever I land—already fixed upon in my mind. I know you very well. Your name's Eselganz—Andreas Eselganz—and you're one of the best hotel touts on the Rhine. But you're wasting your time on me. There are no other English travellers on board, so you'd better have a cigar (which I will give you, if you please) and a glass of Maitrank, or whatever you like, and tell me a story."

"With a hundred thousand pleasures," the man in the sky-blue trousers, who was as placable as he was devoid of shame at a rebuff, replied. " Here, Kellner, a bottle of English beer" [(I declare they charged me three-quarters of a thaler for it, and I believe the tout went halves with the waiter in the plunder); " with gratitude, also, I accept your cigar, which I perceive is of the real Havannah brand. I can sell you any quantity at reasonable rates, warranted genuine, and direct from Cabana's (who is my uncle), in Havannah."

" In Hamburg, you mean?" I resumed. " There, Herr Eselganz, never mind the cigars,

and the bear's-grease, and the Brussels lace, and
the real eau-de-Cologne, which you've always had
to sell any time these ten years. Somebody else
may buy 'em. I won't. Tell me a story; never
mind if it's a true one or not, but tell it for old
acquaintance' sake."

"A story—a story! How curious you English are, and how wise you think yourselves!
By the way, and under correction, you are lying
even now under a grievous mistake. You said
that, save yourself, there were no English on
board."

"There were none, at least, at the table
d'hôte."

"Error, my dear sir, error," said the man in
the sky-blue trousers. "That lady who sat opposite to you was English, and of the highest nobility. Who but Lady Adelaide Mount Ephrom,
the noble Earl of Tunbridge's daughter?" (Escl-
ganz has his Peerage by heart, as might be expected from one who, before he went into boating
business, was one of the most active couriers to

be heard of at the bar of the Leather Bag, in Dover-street, Piccadilly).

"Lady Adelaide Mount Ephrom! She's been dead these five years."

"Not at all," persisted Herr Eselganz. "She is alive, and married to the Swedish Count Boomerangström. Behold her, the blonde daughter of Albion, reading one of the good little books she is so fond of."

I turned and followed the guiding finger of the tout, and there sure enough, on a special camp-stool, was a lady with very long flaxen ringlets, and of a certain age, which means that her appearance suggested not the slightest clue as to whether she was an old fifteen, or a young fifty. She was very fashionably dressed, and was busily engaged in reading; and behind her was her husband, the Swedish count, who, clad in a fawn-coloured coat and white trousers, with a white hat, a very pasty face, a bald head, long blonde moustaches, and eyes inclining to the bloodshot, looked very much as though he had

passed through an imperfect stage of metempsy-
chosis, and had not quite succeeded in obliter-
ating the outward traces of a white mouse.

"Count Boomerangström," whispered my companion, "is, as you are aware, the proprietor of
the great iron mines of Bendigokoping, of which
all your so famous shilling razors are made. But
he is not so rich as his wife. Aha! it is on her
ladyship that the great Schweinsfleisch diamond
is settled.

" The Schweinsfleisch diamond?"

"The same. Kings and emperors have alike
rivalled each other, but in vain, in offers to purchase it. The Hermitage at Petersburg, the
Treasury at Stamboul, your own Tower of London Jewel House, are poverty-stricken without
it. Rothschild is not rich enough to buy it.
Behold it, even in the form of a large brooch, at
the throat of the so well-born British-origined
Gräfinn!"

Again I looked at the Countess Boomerangström, né Mount Ephrom; and sure enough her

chemisette was secured by a magnificent brooch composed of a single brilliant—the largest I had ever seen. In the very centre, however, of the gem was the very unusual addition of what appeared to be a small ruby, tear shaped.

"What is the meaning of that ruby drop?" I asked. "Does it not spoil the lustre of the diamond, when placed there right in its midst!"

"Aha! a ruby, you call it!" chuckled Herr Eselganz. "You wanted a story, and you shall have one, precisely concerning that diamond and its so-called ruby drop. Yet another bottle of English beer; so. A light, thank you." And the man in the sky-blue trousers thus addressed himself to continuous narrative:—

It was in the early part of the eighteenth century (he began) that the Grand-Duchy of Schweinhundhausen, a territory situated as you are aware, geographically accomplished sir, to the north-eastward of the territory of Weissnichtwo, and for its Sovereign Ludwig Adolf the Seventy-fourth, surnamed the Terrible. He was an awful tyrant. The total number of his subjects amounted to about ten thousand, all of whom, from the baby in arms to the alms old woman of eighty, spinning at the almshouse door, hated him with intense cordiality. His family detested him with remarkable unanimity. His eldest son, Prince Ludwig, had been driven into banishment many years before. Opinions were divided as to whether his exile was due to his having knocked down his father for kicking his mother, or to his papa having been detected in sprinkling some pretty white powder, which glittered very much, over the Spartan ration of sauerkraut, which formed the prince's daily and solitary meal. At all events, he had been comfortably tried for high treason in his absence, and executed in effigy; while, to guard against all contingencies, the whipping-post in the market-place of Schweinhundhausen was garnished with a permanent announcement from the grand-ducal and paternal pen, offering a reward of one hundred florins to whomsoever should capture the condemned traitor, Ludwig von Porkstein (the family name of the Princes of Schweinhundhausen), dead or alive. Friedrich Adolf, the second son, and usually known as Arme Fritz, or poor Fred, had merely been turned out of doors at the age of sixteen, and was supposed to be serving as a sergeant in the armies of the Kaiser. Dorothea Adolfina, the eldest daughter, rendered desperate by continual persecution, had run away with Count Putz von Putzenburg, the penniless younger son of a sovereign count, whose family had for centuries been bitter foes to the house of Porkstein. Ludwig Adolf the Seventy-fourth had the fugitive and disobedient princes duly cursed in the court chapel by Ober-Hof-Prediger Dr. Bonassus, and having added his paternal malison thereto, cut her picture to shreds with a penknife, and forbidden her name to be mentioned, under penalty of the pillory and the spinning-house, by any grand-ducal subject, felt comfortable. Of his large family, then, there only remained at the

Residenz of Schweinhundhausen two young prin-
cesses, who were fed on sauerkraut, kept in continual terror, and whipped every Monday morning
by their governess, whether they deserved it or
not; and a very small young prince, named Carl
Adolf, whom, somehow, his cruel father did not
dare to ill treat, for he had his mother's eyes;
and it was only a week before his birth that the
poor grand-duchess (who died *en couches* of little
Carl) had looked with those same eyes (after a
horrible scene in the dining-room of the Residenz) upon Ludwig the Seventy-fourth, and
gasped out: " You are my murderer !" The
ground-down population of Schweinhundhausen
used to say, that this tiny younker was the only
human being in the grand-duchy who dared say
that his soul was his own.

Ludwig Adolf was a prince who did as he liked,
and nearly everything he had a liking to was bad.
Whenever he put on his yellow stockings striped
with black, it was a sign that he meant mischief,
and he put them on at least three times a week.

In his grand court suit of yellow velvet, with the famous stockings to match, his *blood*-coloured ribbon of the Grand-Ducal Order—pray observe the colour—of the Pig and Whistle, and a monstrous white periwig surmounting his swollen and voilet-stained countenance, he indeed merited his sobriquet of the Terrible, and looked like a gigantic wasp crossed with a Bengal tiger. He had an army of one hundred and fifty men, all clothed in flaming yellow striped with black. He beat them unmercifully, but was sometimes capriciously generous, and caroused with them until unholy hours in the dining-hall of the Residenz. He was very fond of gambling, but woe be to the wretch who won money of his Sovereign! He was given to deep drinking, but he had no mercy upon the soldier whose eyes were inflamed, or whose gait was unsteady on parade. To the halberds, the picket, or the black-hole with him at once! He had invented a cat with thirteen tails for the especial torture of his soldiers; but a cane was his famous instrument of correction.

He caned his lackeys, he caned his children (always excepting little Carl), he caned the page who, with his knees knocking together, presented his mid-day beaker of Rhine wine to him; he caned the sentinel at the palace gate, who always had the palsy when he presented arms to Ludwig the Terrible. He would sally forth in the morning with a well-caned aide-de-camp, carrying horror and confusion with him all over Schwein-hundhausen. The mothers hid their children under the bed when his saffron-coloured roque-laure was seen at the end of the street; the girls locked themselves in their bedrooms; the baker felt his oven become icy; the blacksmith shivered at his forge. He would kick over the old women's spinning-wheels and apple-stalls at the street corners. He would burst into the taverns, declare the measures were short, and cause all the beer to be flung into the gutter. He would invade the tribunals, thrust the Staats Procurator from his seat, bully the Assessor, and reverse the sentences, always on the side of severity. A dreadful dumbness, accompanied by a sinking of the heart into the shoes, and a quivering of the lip took place when he entered the schools, and bade the Magister point out to him the worst-behaved boys. Then he would go home to the Residenz and dine on spiced and fiery meats, oftentimes flinging the plates and dishes at the heads of the servants, or kicking his secretary's and chamberlain's shins under the table. He ate like a shark, drank like a hippopotamus, bellowed like a bull, swore like a trooper, and then, until it was time to have a carouse with his yellow-clad warriors, snored like a pig. In short, Ludwig Adolf the Seventy-fourth was an absolute monarch, and there were a great many monarchs as trumpery and as tyrannical as he on these charming Rhine banks in the early days of the eighteenth century.

He was very rich. In fact, when one is absolute and has a good private revenue, augmented by the power of taking what does not belong to one; and, moreover, when one takes a good deal, wealth is a matter of course. How many barrels full of gold Ludwigers, to say nothing of thalers and florins, there were in the cellar of the Residenz, I have never heard; but it was universally agreed that Ludwig Adolf was rich enough to buy all Putzenburg and Weissnichtwo, to say little of the adjoining electorate of Kannnichtsagen, out-and-out.

When your far-seeing British Parliament resolved upon calling the illustrious House of Brunswick to the throne of Great Britain, France, and Ireland, and when, on the death of Queen Anne, the illustrious Kurfurst or Elector of Hanover became George the First of England, mighty dreams of ambition began to course through the heated brain of Grand-Duke Ludwig. He was on friendly terms with the Elector King. He had drank deep, and played deeper still, with him. His majesty had said all kinds of flattering things to him; why not, through that august influence, now powerful in Germania, should not he exchange his duchy

for an electorate, for a kingdom? or rather, why
should he not create one by aggrandising himself
at the expense of his neighbours—Putzenburg,
and Weissnichtwo, and Kannnichtsagen?

"It must be," cried Ludwig Adolf, twisting
his red moustaches—I forgot to tell you that a
pair of red eyebrows, one of red eyelashes, and
one of red moustaches, flamed beneath the white
periwig—"I have said it; I must send my brother of England the Grand Cross of my order of
the Pig and Whistle!"

"Indeed, a sagacious, generous, and truly
grand-ducal thought," murmured Mr. High
Chamberlain Rappfeugel, who was compelled to
come every evening to smoke a pipe and drink
strong waters for some hours in the Presence,
although the poor man drank nothing stronger
than barley-water at home, and the mere odour
of tobacco gave him hideous qualms.

Ludwig Adolf could swallow any amount of
flattery, yet he frowned at this compliment from
the chamberlain. " Grand-ducal, grand-ducal,"

he grumbled between his teeth, " why not kingly warum nicht, oh Grand-Duke of Donkeys?"

Dr. Ober-Hof-Prediger Bonassus, who sat on the other side, and who really liked his pipe, was a better courtier. In a discreet undertone he characterised his sovereign's ideas as "truly imperial." He would have been safe for a bishopric, had there been any episcopate in Schweinhundhausen.

Ludwig Adolf was appeased. "Yes," he continued, "I shall send my master of the ceremonies and introducer of ambassadors"—(no diplomatists were ever accredited to the grand-duchy, but that did not in the least matter)—"Von Schaffundkalben, to London, with the gift to my brother König George. But that you, oh chamberlain, are an incorrigible ass and dunderhead, I would confide the mission to you."

Mr. High Chamberlain bowed. "Your Mansuetude," he ventured to remark, "will doubtless send the much-prized decoration in gold."

"In gold!" thundered Ludwig the Terrible.

" Cow, idiot, blockhead. Thinkest thou I am a pauper, a miser? I shall send it in brilliants. The centre shall be composed of the great Schweins-fleisch diamond. Let Abimelech Ben Azi, the Court Jew, be sent for, to present himself here the first thing on the morrow morning, or it will be the worse for him."

At the mention of the great Schweinsfleisch diamond there was a buzz of amazement mingled with terror among the courtiers. The poor grand-duchess, deceased, had brought this celebrated gem as part of her wedding portion. She had been a princess of Kaltbraten Schweinsfleisch, hence the name of the jewel, which was supposed to be the largest diamond not alone in Germany, but (as the Schweinhundhauseners fondly believed) in all Europe. The surprise, therefore, of the court when they heard that this priceless heir-loom was to be sent as a present to a foreign sovereign, may be easily imagined. Their terror may be accounted for when it is mentioned that the great Schweinsfleisch diamond had ever been held as a jewel of evil omen, bringing misfortune upon all who were in any way concerned with it.

Although Schweinhundhausen was a very small town, it had, like most other Germanic capitals at that epoch, its Jews' street, or Judengasse. There dwelt the few Israelites who contrived to shuffle through existence without being skinned alive by the exactions of Ludwig Adolf; and in the smallest, dirtiest house of the whole Judengasse lived certainly, next to the grand-duke, the richest man in Schweinhundhausen, Abimelech Ben Azi. He dealt in old clothes, watches, money, china, tea and coffee, snuff-boxes, anything you please; but he was also a most expert and accomplished goldsmith and jeweller, and by virtue of the last-named qualifications had been promoted to the rank of Court Jew. Ludwig Adolf was, on the whole, very gracious to Abimelech Ben Azi, condescending to borrow a few thousand florins from him at nominal interest from time to time, not because he wanted the money, but in order to let the Court Jew know that he was, in his normal condition, a person to be squeezed.

On the morrow morning, Abimelech, having been duly summoned by a Court page, made his appearance, not without fear and trembling, at the Residenz; for if there be one thing more disagreeable than being called upon by an absolute monarch, it is having to call upon him. He was received by the high chamberlain, who, as he was in the habit of borrowing his quarter's salary in advance—and Ludwig Adolf always kept his courtiers three-quarters in arrear, and made it high treason to ask for cash—from the Court Jew, was tolerably civil to him. In due time he was ushered into the presence, and made the numerous and lowly obeisances required by Schweinhundhausen etiquette. A cold chill, however, pervaded the spinal marrow of Abimelech Ben Azi when he saw peeping from beneath the dressing-gown of His Mansuetude (flame-coloured taffety embroidered with crimson) those direly renowned yellow stockings which, whenever donned, were assumed to mean mischief.

For a wonder, however, the terrible potentate seemed unusually placable. Little Prince Carl was playing at his feet, quite unmoved by the sight of the flaming legs, and ever and anon Ludwig Adolf would bestow a grin of affection on his youngest born, which would have been positively touching, had it not too closely resembled the leer of a hyæna over some especially toothsome morsel of a shin-bone of beef.

"Mr. Court Jew," said His Mansuetude, "what is the course of exchange?"

Abimelech Ben Azi began to falter out something about thalers, florins, and marks banco, making up his mind that he had been bidden to the presence for the purpose of being squeezed, when Ludwig Adolf stayed him with a gracious movement of his hand. I say gracious, because this prince seldom lifted his hand, save to throw something, or to hit somebody.

"Mr. Court Jew," he pursued, "I have a task for you to perform. That, if you fail in performing it to my satisfaction the skin will be removed from the nape of your neck to the sole of your foot, is, I flatter myself, a sufficient guarantee for your zeal and industry. Dog! it is my desire that you set the great Schweinsfleisch diamond forthwith as a centre to the Grand Cross of the Order of the Pig and Whistle."

To hear, in all matters of business with Ludwig the Terrible, was to obey. Abimelech Ben Azi took away the great diamond with him, not without some remonstrances from little Prince Carl, who wanted to play with it, and hiding the precious bauble beneath the lappet of his gaberdine, returned to his house in the Judengasse. He had been instructed to spare no expense as to the gold for setting, and some minor gems to encircle the great diamond. He was to make it a truly imperial gift. When he reached home it was dinner-time, and his wife and seven children forthwith abandoned their mess of millet and oil, and swarmed round him to gaze upon the wondrous sheen of the great Schweinsfleisch diamond. Jochabad Spass, his long journeyman, saw the diamond too, and grinned an evil grin.

Jochabad Spass had served his apprenticeship at Swederbad, the capital of the principality of Mangel-Wurzelstein. Father or mother he had none. He had an unlovely manner, a cruel eye, and an evil grin; but he was a capital workman, and the right-hand man of Abimelech Ben Azi.

"What a pity that such a beautiful diamond should be sent to the beef-eating Englanders," said the long journeyman.

"Ah! 'tis a pity, indeed," said the Court Jew.

"Not only a pity, but a cruel shame," exclaimed Esther, his wife; an opinion re-echoed by the seven children, who had all loved diamonds from their youth upwards.

"What a pity, too," resumed Jochabad, "that even while here it should lie hidden in the treasury of a cruel old tyrant, instead of making the fortune of two honest merchants."

"Hush, hush!" cried Abimelech; "you are talking treason, *mein lieber.*" But still he lent a greedy ear to what his journeyman said.

"The stone is worth two hundred thousand florins," remarked Jochabad.

"So much?"

"And diamonds, the bigger the better, are *so* easy to imitate by those to whom the real secret has been revealed. Did I not learn it from old Father Schink before I came hither, three years since?"

"*Ach! Himmel!*" cried the Court Jew, in a fright. "Do you want to ruin us, O Jochabad Spass?" But he listened to the tall tempter nevertheless.

He listened and listened until the two agreed together to commit a great crime. The secret of counterfeiting diamonds by means of a fine vitreous paste was then very little known; indeed, it is questionable whether ever artisan attained so great a proficiency in the sophisticatory craft as Jochabad Spass, the pupil of Father Schink. So well did Spass consummate his fraud, that when he showed the false diamond to his accomplice, the Court Jew was himself for a moment deceived, and thought that he was gazing on the veritable gem. The Schweinsfleisch diamond itself was placed in an iron casket, and carefully concealed beneath the flooring of the workshop, the two rogues agreeing to wait until Ludwig Adolf the Seventy-fourth died, or was assassinated, or until they could slip away from his dominions, and sell the stolen jewel in some one of the great European capitals.

In due time the Grand Cross of the Pig and Whistle, with a blazing imposture, glistening with all the colours of the rainbow in its centre, was completed, and taken by Abimelech Ben Azi, not without certain inward misgivings, to the Residenz. But Ludwig Adolf suspected no foul play. It could not enter into his serenely absolute mind that any mortal would dare to play any tricks with him. He was, on the contrary, delighted with the decoration; and was pleased to say that he never thought the great Schweinsfleisch diamond could have looked so well. Thenceforward was the Court Jew in high favour, and was even given to understand by the high chamberlain, that, as a mark of His Mansuetude's gracious bounty, he might be permitted, on His Mansuetude's next birthday, to leave the Judengasse, and purchase for twenty thousand florins an old tumble-down house in the Hof-Kirche-Platz, of which the grand-duke happened to be proprietor.

On the twenty-fourth of August, 17—, Introducer of the Ambassadors and Master of the Ceremonies Schaffundkalben was despatched on his mission. He was graciously permitted to pay his own travelling expenses, but was promised the second class of the Pig and Whistle at his return. As the subjects of the grand-duke had a curious habit of not coming back when they once got clear of the grand-ducal dominions, Ludwig Adolf took the precaution, for fear of accidents, to place Von Schaffundkalben's estates under temporary sequestration, and furthermore to lock up his daughter snugly and comfortably in a community

of Lutheran canonesses. However, impelled by
loyalty and fidelity, quickened, perhaps, by these
little material guarantees, the introducer of ambassadors made his bow again at the Residenz
within four months of his departure. He brought
the warmest and most grateful acknowledgments
from King George the First of England, contained in a letter couched in very bad French,
and beginning "*Monsieur mon cousin,*" and was,
besides, the bearer of two exquisitely hideous
Dutch pugs, an assortment of choice china monsters, a chest of tea, and a dozen of York hams,
as a present from the Majesty of England to the
Mansuetude of Schweinhundhausen. Ludwig
Adolf was slightly wrath that the royal hamper
did not contain a brace of Severn salmon and a
few barrels of Colchester oysters, and was with
difficulty appeased at the representation of his
emissary, that those piscine delicacies would have
lost somewhat of their freshness in the journey
from England.

It is necessary, for a moment, that the scene of

my story should be transferred to the cold and
foggy, but highly respectable, island I have just
named. About that time, in the Haymarket of
London, there was an Italian Opera House called
the King's Theatre. His Majesty King George
contributed a thousand guineas every season in
order to encourage his nobility towards the patro-
nage of that splendid but exotic entertainment.
During the winter season of 17—, the principal
Italian singing woman at the King's Theatre was
the famous Lusinghiera. Her real name was, I
believe, Bobbo; but she was justly entitled to her
sobriquet of the Lusinghiera, for none could
flatter the great, or twist them round her little
finger, as she could. I detest scandal, and it is
therefore sufficient to say that La Lusinghiera
found favour in the eyes of King George, who, if
you remember, had left his lawful wife in Hanover, and was not, owing to that unfortunate
Königsmark affair, on the best of terms with her.
Now, La Lusinghiera was exceedingly fond of
money, likewise of monkeys, and of maccaroni;

but for diamonds she had a positive passion. I
believe that, had she tried her best, she would
have flattered King George out of the crown
jewels, although, constitutionally speaking, they
were not his to give away; but she chose to take
into her capricious head a violent longing for that
part of the Order of the Pig and Whistle which
consisted of the great Schweinsfleisch diamond.
The king often wore it in private—although the
gross Englanders laughed at it—for he loved
every thing that reminded him of Germania. The
Lusinghiera plainly told him that she would give
him no more partridges and cabbage—of which
dish he was immoderately fond—for supper, unless he made her a present of the much-coveted
decoration. He expostulated at first, on the score
of the courtesy due to his cousin of Schweinhundhausen; but La Lusinghiera laughed at him,
and at Ludwig Adolf and his grand-duchy, and
the end of it was that the fatuous king satisfied
her greed.

Partial as the Italian singing woman was to

diamonds for their natural beauty, she did not also
disdain them for their intrinsic value. Her curiosity to know how much the great Schweinsfleisch
diamond was worth in hard cash had speedily an
opportunity of being gratified. It chanced that
she wanted some ready money—say a couple of
thousand guineas. As King George happened to
be at Hampton Court, and she had been tugging
somewhat violently at the royal purse-strings
lately, La Lusinghiera condescended to seek temporary assistance from a financier who was always
ready to grant it on the slight condition of some
tangible security, worth at least three times the
amount, being deposited with him. In fine, she
stepped into her chariot, and was driven to Cran-
bourne-alley, to the shop of Mr. Tribulation
Triball, pawnbroker. There, producing the Order
of the Pig and Whistle from its grand morocco
case, whereon were emblazoned the united arms
of England and Schweinhundhausen ("like the
fellow's impudence," King George had muttered,
when he first opened his cousin's gift), she dwelt

on the beauty of the great Schweinsfleisch diamond, and demanded the sum of which she stood
in need.

Mr. Tribulation Triball was a discreet man, who
asked very few questions in business. He would
have lent money on the great seal of England, or
on the Lord Mayor's mace, had either of those
valuables been brought to him by ladies or gentlemen of his acquaintance. He examined the
decoration very carefully; pronounced the setting
to be very pretty; but, with a low bow, regretted
his inability to advance more than fifty pounds on
the entire ornament.

" Fifty pounds ! " screamed the Lusinghiera in
a rage. " What do you mean, fellow ? "

" I mean, honoured madam," replied the pawnbroker, with another low bow, " that fifty pounds
is very nearly the actual value of the gold and the
small stones; and for fashion, as you are well
aware, we allow nothing."

" Al Diavolo, your fashion ! " exclaimed La Lusinghiera; " I have sacks full of gold brooches

and small stones at home. 'Tis on the pietra grossa, the great diamond, that I want two thousand guineas."

"Which sum I should be both proud and happy to lend," observed the pawnbroker, " but for the unfortunate circumstance that the great centre stone happens to be not worth sixpence. It is false, madam—false as a Brummagem tester."

"False !" yelled La Lusinghiera.

"False," repeated Mr. Triball. "A marvellous good copy, I grant you, but it will not deceive such an old hand as I am. It must be one of the famous paste imitations of Father Schink. However, your ladyship must not go away empty-handed. Let us see whether we cannot arrange a small loan on a note of hand."

I don't know what sum La Lusinghiera managed to borrow from Mr. Tribulation Triball, but it is certain that she did not leave the great Schweinsfleisch diamond with him in pledge. She went home in a rage, and as soon as his Majesty came back from Hampton Court, she had with him what is termed in modern parlance an "explication." A terrible one it was. I don't know which suffered most—his Majesty's feelings or his periwig. However, a reconciliation, very costly to royalty, followed, and La Lusinghiera gave back the worthless Order of the Pig and Whistle.

Let us now return to Schweinhundhausen. It was on the twenty-fourth of August, 17—, precisely twelve months from the day when the Introducer of Ambassadors Von Schaffundkalben had started on his mission, that an English courier arrived at the Residenz, and handed a packet to the high chamberlain, who in turn handed it to His Mansuetude. Ludwig Adolf received it with a smile, and ordered the courier to be sumptuously entertained in the buttery. He came from his cousin of England, and the grand-duke felt certain that he must be the bearer of at least the British Order of the Garter.

Ludwig the Terrible opened the packet, perused

a letter which it contained, and was soon afterwards seen to turn blue. Then he tore open the
inner envelope of the packet and turned crimson.
Then he cast something upon the ground and
trampled it beneath his heel. Then he ordered
his yellow stockings. Then he began to curse and
to kick his pages. Eventually he turned to the
high chamberlain, flung him the letter, and thundered forth, " Read that."

The missive was not from the King of England,
but from his Majesty's principal Secretary of
State for Foreign Affairs, who, in terms of con-
temptuous frigidity, " begged leave to return the
spurious jewel sent to his Britannic Majesty, and
had the honour to remain."

By this time Ludwig the Terrible was foaming
at the mouth. " Spurious," he gasped, " spurious! I see it all. Rascal, robber. Quick,
twelve halberdiers, and let Abimelech Ben Azi,
and the dog who is his journeyman, be brought
hither."

It was about twelve at noon that Jochabad

Spass was smoking his after-dinner pipe—they dined at eleven in Schweinhundhausen—at the door of his master's shop in the Judengasse. He looked up the street and down the street, when suddenly round the corner which gave on to the Hof-Kirche-Platz, he saw two of the yellow and black halberdiers make their appearance. The Court Jew's house was just at the other extremity of the street, and as soon as Jochabad saw halberdiers one and two succeeded by halberdiers three and four, than Jochabad Spass, who, if he were indeed a dog, was a very sly one, slipped round the corner of the opposite extremity of the street.

"Good-by to Schweinhundhausen," he said philosophically, running meanwhile as fast as his legs would carry him. "There is a storm brewing. It will be a bad day for the house-father. What a pity I had not time to secure the casket."

The twelve halberdiers arrived at Abimelech Ben Azi's house, seized upon that unfortunate Israelite, and, notwithstanding the entreaties of his wife and children, bound his hands tightly behind his back. It was the invariable practice of the ministers of the grand-ducal justice, whenever they paid a domiciliary visit, to leave marks of their presence by eating and drinking up everything on the premises. This traditional ceremony was gone through while the wretched Abimelech writhed in his bonds and moaned in terror; and then the guards, placing him in their midst, playfully prodded him up the Judengasse, across the Hof-Kirche-Platz, and so through the avenue of linden-trees to the Residenz.

But he was not received in the Hall of Audience. No; the Hall of Justice was the destination of the wretched man. As a preliminary measure he was taken into the guard-room and loaded with heavy fetters, and then he was dragged down a couple of flights of slimy stairs into this so much dreaded Hall of Justice—a gloomy, underground apartment, supported by massive stone pillars, and illumined only by two grated windows on a level with the pavement of the court-yard. The place was very dark and damp, and if it had been situated in an English mansion, and not in a grand-ducal residence, would have most probably gone by the name, not of a Hall of Justice, but of a coal-cellar.

At the upper end of the hall sat Ludwig the Terrible, in a great crimson arm-chair. Facing him, a few paces distant, was another chair, empty, and behind it stood, mute and grim, a swarthy man in a blacksmith's apron, and with his sleeves rolled up to the elbows, whom the unfortunate Ben Azi knew well to be Hans Dummergeist, sworn scourger, headsman, and tormentor to the grand-duke.

"Good day, Mr. Court Jew," said Ludwig Adolf, with affected courtesy, as the prisoner was brought in tottering between two halberdiers. "What is the course of exchange, Mr. Court Jew?"

The miserable man's lips moved convulsively, but he could articulate nothing.

"What is the price of diamonds?" the grand-duke continued, his voice rising to a yell of derision. "How stands the great Schweinsfleisch diamond quoted in the market?"

The Court Jew made a desperate effort: "The great Schweinsfleisch diamond," he faltered; "did not your highness entrust it to me to set, and did you not send it as a centre-piece of the Grand Cross of the Order of the Pig and Whistle to his Majesty the King of England?"

"Oh, inconceivably mangy and thievish dog," roared Ludwig Adolf, now losing all command of himself, "behold and tremble." And he thrust beneath the nose of the unhappy Court Jew an open leathern case, in which he saw lying, in confused fragments, the decoration he had made, and in its midst, winking with delusive glitter, the spurious diamond.

"Court Jew," continued Ludwig Adolf, with a growl like that of a hungry bear, "you and I will pass the afternoon together. But first, egregious and impudent knave, where is the diamond

—the real diamond—the great Schweinsfleisch diamond you have robbed me of?"

In vain did Abimelech Ben Azi protest that he knew nothing about it, that he had set the real stone as he had been ordered to do, that it must have been taken out, and a false one substituted for it in England; that he was as innocent as the babe unborn. He was, by the command of the grand-duke, bound down in the great arm-chair facing that tyrant, and, to extort confession, the dreadful infliction known as the Osnaburg torture was applied to him. For a long time he held out ; but after three applications of the torture—after the boots had been applied to his legs and the thumbscrews to his fingers, his fortitude gave way, and in scarce audible accents he confessed his guilt, and described the place beneath the flooring of his workshop, where, in its iron casket, the great Schweinsfleisch diamond was to be found. The fury of Ludwig Adolf was still further heightened, when, commanding Jochabad Spass to be brought before him in order that he, too, as with grim facetiousness he expressed it, might make "a journey to Osnaburg," he was informed that the long journeyman had escaped. How he managed it was never known, but from that day Jochabad Spass was never seen in Schweinhundhausen.

Another detachment of halberdiers, accompanied by the high chamberlain, was despatched with chisels and sledge-hammers to the Judengasse, and during their absence restoratives were forced down the throat of Abimelech Ben Azi, who remained still bound to the arm-chair, Ludwig Adolf glaring upon him like a boa-constrictor upon a rabbit.

In half-an-hour's time the messengers returned with an iron casket, which with their united strength they had not been able to break open. The deplorable Court Jew, however, made signs that the key would be found hung round his neck. Search being made, this proved to be the case, and at length the long-ravished gem was placed in the hands of Ludwig the Terrible.

I have heard that the tyrant kissed it, and
fondled it, and called it by endearing names;
then, that, taking the true diamond in one hand
and the false one in the other, he thrust each
alternately beneath the nose of his captive, crying,
" Smell it, Mr. Court Jew, smell it." I have
heard that all the tortures the wretched creature
had already undergone were repeated over and
over again in sheer wantonness; that the false
diamond was heated in a brazier, and, held between pincers, forced into the prisoner's naked
flesh. His screams were appalling. Two of the
halberdiers fainted. Even the sworn tormentor
was heard to mutter "Es ist genug." On being
called upon for an explanation, he replied that he
did not consider the patient could endure any
more without Nature giving way.

" It *is* enough, then," Ludwig Adolf the Seventy-
fourth acquiesced, with a darkling scowl. " Mr.
Sworn Headsman, be good enough to fetch your
sword this way."

At the mention of the word sword, Abimelech

Ben Azi, who had been in a semi-swoon, set up a horrifying yell. In the most piteous terms he besought forgiveness. He essayed to drag himself towards his persecutor, as though to embrace his knees, when, in his frantic efforts, he lost his balance, and the heavy chair fell over on the top of him, as he, still bound to it, grovelled at the feet of Ludwig the Terrible.

" Set him up again !" thundered the merciless prince ; " and, headsman despatch. I'll teach him to steal my diamonds !"

The last dreadful deed was soon done. The headsman brought his long sharp sword—a double-handed one with a hollow blade filled with quicksilver, which, as the point was depressed, ran downwards from the hilt, giving increased momentum to the blow. The headsman was as expert as those generally are who serve absolute monarchs. Grasping the hilt of his weapon with both hands, and inclining his body backwards and laterally, he swept off with one semicircular blow the head of Abimelech Ben Azi. Again the body with its chair fell forward at the feet of the tyrant—the head rolled many paces away, and a cascade of blood sprinkled the faces and dresses of the terrified beholders.

It is said that one blood-drop from this shower fell upon the great Schweinsfleisch diamond, which the grand-duke, as though loth to part with it, still held in his hand. With a horrid laugh he licked the gout from the surface of the stone, and spurning the body of the Court Jew with his foot, stalked upstairs to carouse with his ruffians. When he staggered into his bed-chamber late that night, he put his hand in his pocket to take forth the diamond. It felt wet and clammy, and when he brought it to the light it was dabbled in blood.

On the twenty-fourth of August in every year (concluded Herr Eselganz), every year that has elapsed since that frightful scene in the Hall of Justice at Schweinhundhausen—from sunrise until sunset—a drop of blood stands on that fatal diamond. It has gone through strange vicissitudes, passed through many hands, been an heirloom in many families; but that drop of gore has never failed to make its appearance on the great Schweinsfleisch diamond on the anniversary of the murder of Abimelech Ben Azi, the Court Jew, by Ludwig Adolf the Seventy-fourth, of Schweinhundhausen, surnamed the Terrible.

FLOWERS OF THE WITNESS-BOX.

"THE evidence you shall give, shall be the truth, the whole truth, and nothing but the truth, so help you ——" and with the customary adjuration, which, on my ears, always grates with disagreeable harshness from the thoroughly methodical and indifferent sing-song in which the words are pronounced, A. B. is sworn and proceeds to give evidence. I dare say that he often deposes to more than the truth, and I am afraid as often to less than the truth; but I doubt the frequency of his coming up to the exact exigent standard demanded by his oath. Granting him honest, he may be nervous and irritable, with a confused memory for dates, and an inconvenient knack for remembering only those events or portions of conversation which the gentleman in the wig who is teasing him with questions most devoutly wishes were dismissed from his mind. But, consider the witness sworn. Why, if he be a man, does a fatuous greasy smile generally play about his lips as he mumbles at the ragged dog's-eared book which the usher, with an utter disregard for the fitness of things, has provided from the nearest second-hand book-stall among other "properties" of a court of law? Why, when he is duly sworn, does he ordinarily pass the back of his hand over his lips as though to wipe away the taste of the oath he has just taken? Why, from the beginning to the end of his ordeal in the witness-box, is his hat the bane and burden of his existence? Why is the smoothing of its nap—when it has any—a task which he incessantly pursues? Why is its brim an object to be perpetually plucked and pinched with dubby fingers? Why, if the witness be a lady, does she, in lieu of mumbling or kissing the book, give it a defiant smack that is half a bite—as though it were a Man, and she

meant to stand no nonsense from it ? Why does
the lady-witness commence proceedings by re-
tying her bonnet-strings, or her boa? Why in
the thumb of her left hand glove is there almost
invariably an orifice, disclosing flesh ? Why does
the dandy-deponent, the witness of the upper
Ten Thousand, when he leaves the box, contrive
to stumble over two out of the three steps that lie
between him and the floor of the court ?

Why? Well; because the majority of witnesses are nervous and irritable, you may answer.
But you don't see that greasy fatuous smile any-
where out of a court of justice. The back-handed
movement, the painful pantomime with the hat,
the stumble over the stairs, the hole in the thumb
of the left-hand glove, belong to witnesses exclusively ; and witnesses themselves are, so runs my
theory, a race and type of humanity, apart. Some
babies are born with silver spoons, and others
with wooden ladles, in their mouths. I believe in
an order of children who are born with the ragged
dog's-eared book at their lips, by whose cradle

side the swearing usher stands, and who are brought up as witnesses from the breast.

I have come to be within pistol-shot of forty years of age, and I never was publicly examined in any case, civil or criminal, in my life. And yet I have lived, an 't please you, in a continually simmering vat of hot water. Litigation! Why, I know all the offices in Parchmentopolis, as well as any lawyer's clerk in his second year, and have a whole tin box at home full of bills of costs and green ferret. If the number of processes which have been served upon me were all laid together longitudinally, they would reach — say from Doctor's Commons to old Palace Yard. Law-suits! I have been a party to scores of them. Plaints! Her Majesty's attorney-general has done me the honour to bring three several actions against me in the Court of Exchequer, and still I have never stood up in a witness-box, never kissed the book, twiddled my hat, and been told to look at the jury, to listen to the judge, to pay particular attention to the examining counsel, not forgetting general injunctions to "speak up," and to be careful about what I said, on pain of being committed for contempt, or indicted for perjury.

I will admit that my legal testimony has more than once been called for. What I have known, or what other people chose to take it into their heads that I have known, about the rights and wrongs of certain quarrels, has, from time to time, made many most respectable plaintiffs and defendants anxious to "have me in the box," and to subject the discreetly corked bottle of truth within me, to the action, persuasive or coercive, of the forensic corkscrew. It has never come to anything. I have been subpœnaed over and over again. I have touched that mysterious guinea which the clerk, vegetating, perhaps, on a hopeless five-and-twenty shillings a week, hands to you with a grudging politeness—that guinea which neither looks, nor feels, nor sounds, like other money—and which, Vespasian's axiom neverthe-less, *olet*, for it smells of pounced vellum and japanned tin—that guinea, which, somehow, never seems to have been fairly come by, or legitimately earned, but rather to be of the nature of the demon's arles, and which consequently you make all convenient haste to spend in some wild waste or unholy prodigality. I have a stuffed heron in a glass case at home; I bought it with a subpœnal guinea. I bought a chance in the Art-Union with another. I divided a third between a share in the Frankfort lottery, and a box of pills warranted to cure all diseases, and the consumption of which added about half a dozen to the ailments from which I was already suffering. It is, abstractedly, so monstrous and prodigious a thing that the law should pay you anything, that the primary fact of the donative begets recklessness and mistrust. You feel, either that you are taking the money of the widow and the orphan, or that you are the stipendiary of a rogue.

With numerous subpœnas, how is it that the usher has never called my name in court? If litigants have been so anxious to " have me in the box," how comes it that I have never appeared in the box? Let fate and my destinal star reply. Time after time have I gone down to Westminster Hall, to Guildhall, nay, to Croydon or Guildford, when an astute and pennyless plaintiff, wishing simply to annoy a wealthy defendant, has laid the venue of a twenty-pound plaint in Surrey or elsewhere, as far away from the real scene of dispute as possible. Days have I wasted, and waited for the particular case I have been concerned in, to come on; yet, like a boastful but craven pugilist, it never has come on—at least, it has never advanced to sufficient ripeness for my advent to become an event. Either the jury have in an early stage of the case shown unmistakable signs that they had had enough of it, or the judge has suggested an arrangement, complimenting the parties on their high respectability :—when the plaintiff was fully prepared to show that the defendant was twin-brother to Barabbas; whereas the defendant was bent on calling *me* to prove that the habitual turpitude of the plaintiff ex-

ceeded, on the whole, that of Jonathan Wild,
Sawney Bean, and Mother Brownrigge. Likewise is it due in justice to the bar of England to
confess that many of my cases in Westminster
Hall have been settled without going into court,
through the kind offices of the counsel employed
on either side. Who would imagine that so
much benevolence lurked beneath those spiky
horschair wigs; that beneath those austere stuff
gowns such kindly hearts were beating? "Can't
we come to a friendly understanding?" says
Rubasore, Q.C., whom I always (quite erroneously,
it seems) assumed to be a most quarrelsome fellow.
"Come now, my good sir," puts in Serjeant
Squallop, "is there no way of settling this unpleasant little difference?" How glibly they talk
of the uncertainty of the law! How delicately
they hint at the inconvenience of one's private
affairs being sifted before a ribald audience, and
exposed next day in the newspapers! How deftly
they draw our attention to the fact that one story
is a good one till another is told; that, strong

as we may think our case, the other side may have a stronger; that even if we gain a verdict, we may be beaten in the long run by a point of law and a new trial. "And you know what casuists we lawyers are," simpers Rubasore, Q.C., with deprecatory shrug. So the case is settled, and I get my guinea for nothing. Who shall accuse the bar, after this, of a disposition towards fomenting litigation and engendering strife? I wonder if ever I could be a peacemaker. Yes; I think I could, if I were a Q.C. in good practice, with my fee paid beforehand. I think I should be glad to patch up little differences without going into court, if I wanted to get away early to a dinner at Richmond, or if my cob were waiting to take me for an airing, or if I had rather a heavy case coming on in the King's Bench in half an hour, which rendered this particular one in the Common Pleas somewhat of a bore.

I can't say that I am much the better for the gratuitous guineas I have had as compensation for the writ of subpœna; for the stuffed heron is getting rather shaky about the legs, and at the sale of my effects will fetch, I apprehend, something considerably under a crown. But my wanderings in legal purlieus have not been, perhaps, wholly barren. I have studied witnesses, I have marked their ways, made notes of their demeanour, envisaged their lineaments, and catalogued their apparel. I have grown at last — errors excepted, of course — to distinguish witnesses from other men.

You may tell your witness, first, from the fact that he is always hungry and thirsty, and that the voracity with which he partakes of refreshment is equalled by his cheerful alacrity to be fed. For, the witness is a creature to be paid, and not to pay. Nothing edible or potable comes amiss to him. He is ready for a mutton chop, at ten thirty; for a quiet crust of bread and cheese and a glass of old ale—he is very fond of old ale—at noon; for a substantial "point" steak, a mealy potato like a ball of flower, a pickled walnut, and a pint of Allsopp's draught, at one P.M.; for any

number of sandwiches and glasses of sherry
while the managing clerk holds him in whispered
confabulation as to that one point about which
he is to be so very particular in giving his evidence, and which he either totally forgets, or
makes some transcendental blunder about, before
he has been five minutes in the box. Then, again,
he is ready, when the case is over, for a regular
good dinner washed down by champagne and port
—the last a peculiar rich brown fruity vintage,
like liquid plum-pudding with plenty of brandy in
it: the special growth of the vineyards patronised
by legal hotel-keepers, and which has the curious
property of causing every witness after the second
glass to inform his neighbour in a confidential
hiccup that if it hadn't been for the manner in
which he gave his evidence, the case would have
infallibly broken down. The miscreant Stradlings would have won the day, and the noble-
hearted Styles — who gives the dinner — would
have been nowhere. It is, in fact, in these legal
hotels that witnesses may literally be said to live

on the fat of the land. They are not proud.
While better viands are getting ready they will
make shift with a basin of mock-turtle, in which
scraps of glutinous parchment appear to have
been boiled in lieu of calves'-head. They will
fill up an odd corner with a quarter of a pork-
pie and half a pint of stout; nay, I have even
seen teetotal witnesses (who are generally incoherent in the box, and virulently suspected of
intoxication by the judge) punish the plaintiff's
pocket pretty heavily in the way of Banbury
cakes and lemonade. Country witnesses, whose
stomachs are unused to waiting, and to whom
kickshaws are as the idle wind which they
regard not, are not above taking a substantial lunch from the joint at the Exchequer
dining-rooms; and as for by-drinks, and "quiet
drains," and a cozy pipe and a glass of something hot till that interminable trial of Hudge
versus Gudge shall give place to the long-ex-
pected case of Stradlings versus Styles, their
name is legion. Of course there are, from time

to time, stingy plaintiffs, and pauper plaintiffs, and attorneys who are chary in disbursing costs out of pocket. In these cases the witnesses don't live on the fat of the land, and injure the plaintiff's case accordingly; but there is one repast they must have by fair means or by foul —the first being understood that they are paid for, the second that they pay. They will have tea. The consumption of that refreshing and uninebriating beverage does not in the slightest degree interfere with their appetite for stimulants; still a witness without his tea is nothing. He takes it at all times between noon and five P.M.; but his tea he must and will have: a complete and perfect tea—not a mere cup of wishy-washy Souchong, but supplemented by rounds of toast—the greasier the better—and a rasher of bacon, an egg, or an anchovy, by way of relish. The witness is generally a stranger in the land: he may have come from remote Camberwell, and his tea reminds him of his happy home. The young lady attendant at the

coffee-shop is usually aware of her customer
being a witness, by his asking for the Morning
Advertiser, which organ is not often taken in
under the tea dispensation, and next by his
subsiding into the placid perusal of the Standard of the day before yesterday. He reads of
bygone trials and witnesses of the past, and
buoys himself up, perchance, with the hope that
his own fame will be wafted down to posterity
by the Standard of to-morrow.

The witness, while he is in the chrysalis or
grub state—I mean no pun—but his transition
condition, before he develops into the full-grown
butterflydom of the box, is lifted several hundred feet above his ordinary social altitude. He
lives in another world. He has associates and
intimates he would not have dreamt of being
gregarious with, two days ago. He is made
much of. He is a superior being. Barristers
walk up and down Westminster Hall, arm in
arm with him. Wealthy solicitors clap him on
the shoulder, and tell him to stand firm. Baronets

press his hand, and sometimes leave substantial tokens of their affection for him behind the pressure. Landlords are enjoined to take the utmost care of him. Pale-faced runners from the attorney's office are affected to his service, partially as body servants, partially as spies and guardians, to take care that he does not run away, that he does not throw himself into the arms of the other side; and while they pamper him like a prize-pig, to prevent him from eating and drinking himself into a state of blind oblivion of his duties towards Stradlings and against Styles. For witnesses are mortal men, even as voters at contested elections are, and will sometimes fade away from the paths of prudence. By the way, now that I think of it, the witness, generically speaking, is almost identical in manners, custom, countenance, and conversation, with the voter! And voters are, like witnesses, a species of humanity typical and peculiar in their characteristics. I once had a vote for the county, but I never voted. I was made aware of being seised of a vote for some chambers in town, by the Radical party (my own, oh bitter scorn!) "fighting the battle of the constitution in the Registration Courts," and objecting, on some technical ground, to my qualification. They gained the day, but the victory was disastrous to them, as they had acted (aha!) under the erroneous impression that I was a red-hot Tory; but I humbly thank the revising barrister for striking my name off the register. What should I have done with a vote? Does it concern you, or me, or any other man, in the present pure and healthy state of the political atmosphere, save the regularly stamped, approved, and typical voter, whether Sir John Grampus or General Bounce be the man for Westminster?

There are times when the witness rises to the dignity of a public character; but it is more frequently in connection with an election petition before a parliamentary committee than as a witness in one of the courts at Westminster, that he becomes remarkable. Take Giles Jolter, for instance, assistant-ostler at the Red Herring on Horseback, Chumpsford. The defeated candidate for the representation of that important borough in parliament has petitioned against the sitting member. It is the old story: bribery, corruption, treating, intimidation, and the rest of it. The lawyers on both sides rub their hands and chuckle; for it is a fat case, which, on a moderate computation, will cost about fifty pounds an hour during hearing. Giles Jolter is brought, to his intense amazement, and for the first time in his life, from Chumpsford to London by express train. With him, perhaps, also as witnesses, may be Mr. Chawchobbs, landlord of the Pickled Egg beer-shop, and two or three other agricultural worthies in hobnails and fustian. They all live on the before-mentioned fat of the land. They are in a continual state of beatitude, arising from unlimited feeds of bran-mash, oilcake, and scientifically-sliced mangel-wurzel. They might have

Revalenta Arabica, Thorley's food, Indian pig-meal, for the asking for. They wax fat and kick, and their bones are full of marrow. One of the pale-faced runners, selected for the post on the ground of his being a man about town, is detached to show them the sights and the lions of London. At theatres you may see Chawchobbs fast asleep, with his head leaning on his arms, in the upper boxes. It would never do to take a valuable witness to the pit. At music-halls Giles Jolter's horse-collar grin pervades the stalls. He thinks the Perfect Cure the greatest terpsichorean marvel of the age, yet still offers to back himself for "half a poond" to "joomp agin him." He speculates upon the number of pints of ale consumed by "Any Other Man," preparatory to his stump oration; and at night, when he returns to his lodgings, disturbs the whole house with unearthly yelps and rumblings, in his attempt to imitate the pleasing melody of In the Strand—the Strand. Nothing is spared, in short, to make Giles Jolter's witness-life a car-

nival of joy—this poor conscript of toilsome hus-
bandry, who at home fares worse than the
horses he helps to tend, and has but the Union
to look forward to when his joints have grown
too stiff for his task of currycombing and rubbing
down!—but the scheme of his revelry has one
curious omission. The lawyers have forgotten the
requirements of Jolter and his comrades in the
way of clothes. Chawchobbs has been snatched
in haste and shirt-sleeves from his beer-shop bar,
and when, in places of fashionable or convivial
town resort, you come upon rough uncouth men
of peasant mien, clad in short smoke-frocks,
fustian suits, billicock hats, monumental ankle-
jacks, with rural clay scarce uncaked from them,
and wonderful velveteen waistcoats, with double
rows of mother-o'-pearl buttons, you may be
tolerably certain that a great election petition is
on at Westminster, and that these are witnesses.

It comes to the turn of Giles Jolter to be examined. 'Tis not much he has to prove. Perhaps

he only overheard the conversation in which the sitting member offered the head-ostler (who had a vote) nineteen guineas for a single hair out of the bay mare's tail; or perhaps he found three five-pound notes in the corn-chest, with " Vote for Peverill" on a scrap of paper pinned thereto ; or it may be he was instructed carefully to way-lay, discreetly to kidnap, and completely to fuddle Boolwang, the great radical of Chumpsford. As a rule, the parliamentary committee can make nothing of Giles Jolter. When he is probed for facts bearing on the case, he retails in the Bœotian dialect, scraps of local scandal, damaging to county families of the highest standing.

Thus: Rubasore, Q.C. "Do you remember the thirteenth of June?"

To him Jolter : "Ay, sure-lye, 'twas t' day Squire Gargoyll laid t' horsewhip 'cross uns woife's shouthers i' the coach-house."

At a subsequent period of cross-examination, Serjeant Squallop takes Jolter in hand.

"You say you saw Sir Norman Peverill at

the Red Herring on Horseback. What was he doing?"

"*He wor toight.*"

" What do you mean, sir?"

" Whoy, droonk, tibby sure."

And the unequivocating Jolter bestows the horse-collar grin on the entire auditory (including Sir Norman Peverill, who sups at his club on a rusk and a glass of Seltzer water), in humorous amusement at the simplicity of the learned serjeant, who does not know the meaning of the word " toight."

Not unfrequently Jolter himself appears, as he expresses it, " toight as a droom," and contemplates the august tribunal through a dense haze of beer. He has, in these cases, slipped away from his legal guides, philosophers, and friends, and, wearied with vinous and spirituous luxuries, betaken himself to a rustic orgie of four-penny ale in some Westmonasterian beer-shop, reminding him of his native Bœotia, in company with a sweep, a navigator, and two militia-men.

Sometimes, in these moments of beery abandonment, he is pounced upon by a wary recruiting-sergeant, and forthwith enlisted in her Majesty's Forty-fourth Foot. More than once have parliamentary agents been compelled to pay "smart money" for the ransom of Giles Jolter.

By this time the assistant-ostler has become a public character. He wakes one morning with a headache, and finds himself famous. "No more flagrant instance of the innate and incurable rottenness of our electoral system could be found, we think, than in the hideous tergiversation of the witness Jolter, in his evidence before the committee on the Chumpsford election petition" —thus commences a leading article in a daily newspaper, and G. is the hero of the first paragraph.

Matters, however, may grow serious, and the communicativeness of Giles may become as compromising as his reticence is embarrassing. At all hazards, the assistant-ostler must then be got out of the way, and his cross-examination is cut short by his sudden disappearance. He is spirited away nobody knows whither. Of course the sitting member, and those eminent and astute parliamentary agents, Messrs. Weasle, Eylet, and Hole, are entirely ignorant of his whereabouts. Quick! a proclamation, two proclamations, half a dozen proclamations, for the apprehension of Giles Jolter! It passes comprehension, but it is still within the range of possibility, that the passenger in a blue cloak, with a fur collar, green spectacles, and a sealskin cap, who took the mail train from London to Pangbourne on such a night, was the recalcitrant Giles; nay, he has been seen, with no disguise at all, but in his normal fustian and hobnails, astounding the fisher-girls at Boulogne or Dunkirk with the horse-collar grin. Then Giles is caught, and makes his appearance, quaking and blubbering, at the bar of the House of Commons, where, imagining in his perturbation that he is in peril for poaching, he piteously assures their honours' worships that he " niver tooched a rabbit in uns loife." The end of it is, that after the serjeant-at-arms—to the ineffable disgust of that courtly and bag-wigged functionary —has had charge of Giles for a day or two, he is committed to Newgate under the Speaker's warrant. And there the governor doesn't know what to do with him; and after a few week's incarceration, during which the Sunday papers write about him as a "martyr to oligarchical tyranny," the session comes to an end, and the Speaker's warrant, being by this time so much waste paper, Giles Jolter is discharged. Perhaps a subscription is opened for him in the columns of some red-hot journal, and the first week's list of contributions comprises: "A Foe to Despotism, 5s.;" "Brutus Britannicus, 2s. 6d.;" "Blood or the Ballot, 1s.;" "One who hates M.P.s, 9d. (weekly)," and so forth.

But Jolter subsides, and goes back to Bœotia and Chumpsford to tend his cattle, and is no more heard of. The great tribe of witnesses must submit to a similar fate. Their fame is but ephemeral. Their notoriety endures but for a day. They fade into nothingness and oblivion; in the great crowd they pass unnoticed; and it is only when you hang about the law courts and wear out, wearily, your shoe-leather in the Hall of the Lost Footsteps, that you single them out again, and watch their ways, and dive into their haunts. I never take up the report of a trial twenty years old, without wondering what has become of all the witnesses. What a noise they made in the world, and into what complete forgetfulness they have drifted! As I lay down my pen, an Italian organ-grinder in the street beneath strikes up " Il balen." Confound those organ-grinders! Yet, stay, the brown stranger may be worth studying. Why, goodness, gracious! the name of his papa may have been Theodore Majocchi, that witness of witnesses; and the air ground on the paternal organ, not " Il balen," but " Non mi ricordo ! " His father may have been a witness against Queen Caroline.

BRIGHT CHANTICLEER.

It must have happened to most reasonable persons who have practically studied the "Trivia" of Mr. John Gay, and have endeavoured to adapt its maxims to common use in the difficult feat of walking the streets of London, to have made a miserable mistake in the attempt to accomplish a short cut from the Strand to Oxford Street, and after some hours of desperate and frantic marchings and countermarching, to discover themselves hopelessly and irretrievably lost in Seven Dials. I ought to be tolerably well up in my Dials, for I lived in Great Saint Andrew Street, once; yet I declare that I never yet knew the exact way in or out of that seven-fold mystery. There is always one thing wanting to solve the

topographical enigma. My first, my second, and
so on—up to my sixth—inclusive, of this charade
of streets, I have, after long years of study and
experience, mastered; but my seventh is yet in
the limbo of things unknown; and, for want of
it, I can't unravel the riddle of Seven Dials at
all. So have I known, and know. I know a
most estimable young married lady who has an
admirable recipe for plum-pudding; ay, and
could make it as admirably, but for one little
thing. What that little thing is—salt, sugar,
spice, an egg the more, or a table-spoon of flour
the less—she, I, no one can tell,—but for the
want of the one little thing unknown the pudding
is invariably spoilt—to the casting of gloom over
Christmas and the overflowing of tears from the
hostess. Many of the delicious condiments stick
to the cloth, and what does come to table of the
meritorious, because the well-meant pudding is a
stodgy mass of geology boiled soft—the clayey
formation very apparent, and the red sandstone
uppermost.

Supposing the peripatetic to have well lost himself in Seven Dials; supposing him to have paraphrased the famous "water" line in the Ancient Mariner, and to have cried out, despairingly—

> " Dials, dials, everywhere,
> And not a street I know."

Supposing him to have addressed himself for information successively to a policeman, a costermonger with a barrow, a woman with a black eye, a boy with a sack round him (and nothing else), and a man whose presence is perceptible more by the sense of smell than by that of sight, and who is too drunk to do anything but stand in the middle of the Dials. Supposing him to have been told to move on, to have been mocked, cursed, hooted, and to have had one oystershell and one turnip-stalk cast at him by way of reply, and supposing him, finally, to have become so wearied and dispirited with the noise, the dirt, the smell, the horrible labyrinth he has wandered into, and the howling fiends that come dancing

and fighting from it, that he feels half inclined
to throw himself under the wheels of the fire-
engine that comes tearing by (there always is a
fire—when there isn't a murder—going on in the
vicinity of Seven Dials), or to rush into any one
of the seven gin-palaces that stare at him like
seven Acherons, and drink himself to madness
with vitriolic acid and coculus indicus; this
desirable state of things being arrived, and state
of mind attained, I beg to offer to the peripatetic
a friendly remedy against suicide or insanity.
He will find solace, amusement, and instruction
in the contemplation of " cocks." Seven Dials
is the birth-place and home thereof, and abounds
with them.

Now, a cock is a lie. It is, however, so far
different from and above simple mendacity, that
to succeed, it must be a lie pictorial, a lie literary,
a lie poetical, a lie political, or a lie dramatic.
And it must be, above all things, a lie typo-
graphical; for an unprinted Chanticleer is a mere
rumour, that brings profit to no one; whereas,

printed, it is sold for a halfpenny, and brings bread into the mouth of the seller.

In all the streets and off-streets that pullulate round the Dials—in every shabby slum by night and by day,—in the midst of the fried fish, the dubiously fresh herrings, the radishes, onions, inferior bread, tainted meat, penny looking-glasses, tin Dutch-ovens, ragged children, hulking men, beaten women, drunken everybody; cabbage-leaves, dead cats, mud-carts, garbage, gin-cholera, typhus and death,—to the cultivation of all which, animal and vegetable products, the soil of Seven Dials is wondrously favourable—there are to be found, surrounded by admiring and attentive audiences, certain shabby men, known as patterers, long song sellers, street ballad-singers, dealers in cocks. There is a sallow artist with a blue, bristly beard. He is clad in an absurd masquerade costume of patched, faded drugget, one side of which is gray and the other yellow. The entire suit is plentifully sprinkled with a coarse embroidery of broad arrows, letters,

and numbers. A vile felt hat, of the approved
Woolwich or hulk pattern, covers his head (which,
with a view to further effect, is closely cropped),
and to his ankles are attached a pair of jingling,
clattering fetters. The whole of this picturesque
habiliment is supposed to represent that of a
convict; and the convict himself gives out with
stentorian, though somewhat rusty, lungs a reci-
tation partly in prose, partly in verse, of the
Orrors of Transportation; being the Sufferings of
me William Cockburn condemned unjustly (cela
va sans dire) to be banished from his native
country, serving for life in Chains in the Ulks in
Norfolk Island with my Dangers from Savages
and Wild Beestes and the Cruelties inflicted on
him by order of the British Ministers. Some of
the orrors of transportation and the sufferings of
the ill-used William Cockburn are depicted in
water colours, most vilely, upon a placard stuck
on a pole, bannerwise, which he carries in his
hand. On the placard you may see ferocious
dragoons spearing William Cockburn with lances,

while ruthless grenadiers in scarlet prod him behind with fixed bayonets. In one compartment, the miserable William is represented undergoing the Horrid Punishment of the Lash: the cat having at least nine times nine tails, and the blood spouting from the back in a perfect cascade of crimson. In another, fierce savages, black and decorated with bells, catch William Cockburn, and cook him in a pot and eat him; in another, the dreadful wild beestes career about the wilds of Norfolk Island, desperately clinging to a palm-tree in the midst. Among the wild beestes there are blue lions, tigers of a fiery scarlet hue, and many other infuriated animals whose conformation almost induces the supposition that the griffin is not yet extinct, that the unicorn is yet to be found in the Australian latitudes, and that the dragon of Wantley has removed to and flourishes in Norfolk Island. William Cockburn carries a pile of printed papers, in which the horrors and sufferings he has endured are neatly set forth for family reading.

The type, it must be acknowledged, is somewhat damaged, somewhat broken, and now and then, for a phrase or two, wanting altogether. William's style is diffuse without eloquence, and satirical without humour; but the price is only one halfpenny, and the convict is surely worthy of his hire.

The audience who surround the sufferer are variously affected towards him. Some (the female portion especially) express their opinion that it is "a shame," and ejaculate " poor fellow!" The boys venture conjectures as to " what it was fur?" and how he managed to effect his escape; many of a misanthropic turn of mind pronounce the whole transaction " gammon "—but buy a halfpennyworth, notwithstanding; while one individual who stands a little aloof, chewing the cud of reflection and a flower-stalk—a gentleman whose jacket is of velveteen, greasy; whose trousers are of corduroy, also greasy; whose neck is of the bull's, whose mouth of the mastiff's, whose eye of the wolf's; about whose breast-pocket there is a

certain bulging, as if he kept his life-preserver
there; this gentleman says nothing; but, as
William Cockburn descants upon the horrors of
transportation, he softly whistles, and I really
think he could if he chose tell William Cockburn
a few things concerning Woolwich, broad arrows,
fetters and bayonets, which would astonish him.
I think, too, that he could produce a more interesting piece of reading than one of William's
halfpenny cocks, in the shape of an unpretending
parchment document, which Lord Viscount Pal-
merston has taken the trouble to sign and the
Chief Inspector of Prisons to endorse, and which
is commonly known as a ticket, and of leave.
And I think that the policeman who comes up all
at once like a sirocco, and scatters the whole
assemblage—William Cockburn, fetters, banner,
and audience and all—to the four winds, shares
my opinion; for he looks at the flower chewer,
and the flower chewer looks at him, and so takes
his life-preserver, his ticket of leave, and himself
down an infamous alley, and is seen no more.

While the fetters of Cockburn the transported jingle away into the extreme distance, another dealer starts up on the opposite side of the way. Banner, water-coloured cartoons, pile of papers: he has all these; but he is simply clad in a shabby suit of black, and wears nor fetters, nor particoloured prison dress. A red nose, in passing, I may remark, is common to the whole confraternity. The man in black is bellowing forth the recital of the horrid, cruel, and barbarous murder of a clergyman and five children by gipsies in the north of England, all for one halfpenny. In the next street another banner, another pile of paper, and a Seven Dials Demosthenes in the midst of a philippic on some curious passages in the life of the Reverend Mr. B—— and the widow of General S——, with the whole of the correspondence between the parties; only one halfpenny. Some half dozen yards from him may be another industrial, declaiming the particulars of the Dreadful Assassination of a Lieutenant in the Navy by a young Lady of Quality whom he had deceived and deserted—the perfidious lieutenant being represented in the ordinarily violent water-colours, as receiving his death-blow from the explosion of a pistol, held by the young lady, who is in pink satin with many flounces. Further on, we have Revelations of High Life in connection with the late Mysterious Affair, by the unfortunate Earl of C——; an imaginary conversation between the Pope of Rome and the Earl of Aberdeen, and one between the Emperor of Russia and the Devil. Further on again, a full account of the late serious Catastrophe between a certain Judge and a well-known Countess; Death-bed Confession of Doctor Richard G——; and Awful and feariocious cruelty of a Mother in humble life, attaching black beetles confined in walnut shells upon the eyes of her four young children, and in that state sending them out to beg in the public streets: these, all illustrated by the water colours on the banners, mostly interspersed with snatches of doggerel verse and hoarse melody, and all price one halfpenny, are among the thousand

and one bright chanticleers that form the Seven
Dials day and night entertainments.

Now, all these chanticleers, the crowing whereof
you may hear any time you happen to lose your
way in Seven Dials, and with which, to a smaller
extent, you may be favoured in most of the back
streets—in Clare, Newport, and Portman Mar-
kets; in Holborn, Leather Lane, the Brill at
Somers Town, Tottenham Court Road, the New
Cut, and the Waterloo Road—are all egregious,
barefaced falsehoods. The lieutenant in the navy
has been assassinated by the young lady of quality any time these twenty-five years; the unfortunate Earl of C—— is the unfortunate earl of
nowhere; the story of the Reverend Mr. B——
and the widow of General S—— is as old and
as trustworthy as that of the unfortunate Miss
Bailey and her garters; the death-bed confession
dates from the time of the Princess Charlotte's
death; and William Cockburn probably never
suffered any greater judicial inflictions than were
comprised in an occasional month upon the

treadmill as a rogue and vagabond. The public
—particularly the Seven-Dials public—must
always have some excitement. It is fond of a
good war; it is fonder still, much fonder, of a
good murder; it does not turn up its nose at a
shipwreck or a fire, when the particulars are
sufficiently horrifying, and the number of lives
lost sufficiently numerous. But the public cannot always be accommodated with a good war,
murder, shipwreck, or fire. It will sometimes
happen that nations will shake hands, and individuals with the bump of destructiveness will
refrain from cutting up their near relatives, and
sending them off, packed in tarpaulin, by railway.
Ships do sometimes reach their destinations
without any tribulation to the underwriters at
Lloyds', and Captain Shaw, chief of the London
Fire Brigade, is now and then enabled to enjoy
a peaceable night's rest. Then, the unfortunate Earl of C——, is roused from his slumbers
in a back garret; the naval officer who used the
young lady of quality so cruelly, is deservedly put

once more to the torture of the printing-machine, and worked off into so many quires; the inhuman mother again places walnut-shells, with live black beetles in them, upon the eyes of her helpless children, as she has been accustomed to do on and off during the last half-century; and the barbarous and cruel murder of the clergyman in the North of England is repeated.

The inhabitants of the Dials never seem to become tired of these absurd figments. To some old and middle-aged Dialists, the stories, the doggerel verses, the wretched daubs on the banners, must have been familiar since they were little children; yet to them the monstrosities shouted forth by the hoarse voices of the patterers, seem always as welcome, though quite as stale, as the threadbare jokes of Mr. Merryman, the clown at the circus. I have studied Seven Dials in their connection with patterers these fifteen years durant; and I am of opinion that the older the cock the more it is admired. It takes a long time for a new thing to impress itself upon the Seven Dials mind. Soap, although patent, is scarcely yet recognised in that district. Water is yet looked upon in the light of a frivolous innovation, and clean shirts are regarded as new-fangled inventions. Thus it is in more places than Seven Dials. Tradition, ridiculous, obsolete, barbarous, hurtful as it may be, is ever looked upon with some sort of reverence and affection; and the good old joke, the good old cesspool, the good old tax, the good old job, the good old gallows, and the good old times, abandoned, and are called good because they are pertinaciously retained or reluctantly are old.

Thus, though a printed broadsheet with a full and particular account of the capture of Fort Sumter, the assassination of the Emperor of the French, or the blowing up of the New Houses of Parliament by some modern Guy Fawkes, might cause a transitory excitement in the Dials; while a few new steps might be hewn out of Parnassus by a doggerel ballad upon some passing subject— the Diallian interest will always be found to

revert to the old murders and ballads. The
day passes, these chanticleers pass not away.
Fresh assassins are hanged month after month;
but the last dying speech and confession of John
Thurtell or William Corder still continue to serve
for the valediction of every murderer executed.
Seven Dials are eminently conservative. Sam
Hall only found favour in their eyes because he
was hanged as far back as the reign of Queen
Anne (and it is possible that even then the
ruffianly sweep was only a hash up of some foot-
pad of the reign of James the First). Willikins
and his Dinah are tolerated in the Dials as a
popular melody; but the veterans of the neigh-
bourhood know the song to be as old as the hills.
Lord Bateman and the Fair Sophia flourished in
front of those houses of seven times seven gables,
long before Mr. George Cruikshank undertook to
illustrate the life of that roving nobleman who
employed the proud young porter; and the germ
of Lord Lovell and his milk-white steed was
sprouting in the poetic garden of the Dials, years

before the present favourite singers of that legend were born.

The water-colour placards are all manufactured, the half-penny broadsides all printed, in the immediate vicinity of Seven Dials; and from the mysterious recesses of the courts and alleys round about sally forth the men with the red noses, the hoarse voices, and the shabby clothes, who address the mixed audiences of the Dials. But it will sometimes happen that business (a robbery, a fire, or a razzia on an overturned fruit barrow) or pleasure, such as a mad-dog to hunt, an idiot to hoot and pelt, an accident to follow, a newly-opened public-house to visit, or a favourite fried-fish shop to fight outside of; or temporary satiety—leading the Dialists to lean moodily against posts, or gamble secretly at knuckle-down or poker behind hoardings and piles of bricks, or gaze misanthropically into yawning sewers—will bring chanticleers into considerable depreciation and discount for a time, and cause an almost total dearth of the harvest of halfpence which the patterers strive so hard to reap. Then do these industrious men fly the regions of the Dials, and betake themselves to work the districts inhabited by those favoured ones of humanity—the nobs at the West-end. The stories, however, which would attract admiration and coppers in the Dials would not be quite suitable for Eaton Place or Lower Grosvenor Street. It would scarcely be consonant with delicacy to trumpet forth the misfortunes of the Earl of C—— opposite to the mansion possibly inhabited by his Lordship; and, however merited may have been the revenge taken by the young lady of quality upon the person of the dastardly lieutenant who had destroyed her illusions and blighted her existence, it would scarcely be prudent to allude to the circumstances in the vicinity of the residence of the parents of (perhaps) the young lady of quality herself. So the bill of fare is altered. About nine or ten o'clock in the evening have you never heard, in the silent aristocratic streets, the voices of the patterers calling forth in so-

norous, almost sepulchral accents, accounts of
pestilence, battle, murder, and sudden death :
the assassination of this emperor, the storming of
a certain fortress, accompanied of course, by a
dreadful massacre ? For observe, though personal
reflections upon the aristocracy do not go down
among the nobs at the West-end, horrors are
always sure of a sale. The inhuman mother with
the black beetles is a great favourite in the areas
—that sober insect, the beetle, coming familiarly
home to the serving man and woman's mind in
connection with the kitchen dresser and the coal-
cellar—and ofttimes, as a patterer dwells, with
grim minuteness, upon the horrible perticklers of
the murder; or the agonies of the small children
under the walnut-shells; or, as with grisly unc-
tion he describes Varsaw in flames; the Kezar's
hanser to the Hemperer; war to the last rubble
and the last knife; the Lancashire distress hended
in blood, the hartillery called out; or (a very
favourite device), feariocious hattempt upon her
Majesty by a maniac baker; you will see John

the footman, or Mary the housemaid, steal up the
area steps and into the street, purchase a halfpennyworth of dire intelligence, which, shallow
cock as it is, is read with trembling eagerness and
enthralled interest, in kitchen or servants' hall,
till the cat puts her back up by the fire, and the
hair of the little footpage stands on end. The
shabby men with the solemn voices who peram-
bulate the West-end streets at nightfall are own
brothers to, if not the very same eloquent individuals who carry the banners in Seven Dials; and
they again are descendants of the old flying
stationers, the pleasant lying vagabonds who were
wont to waken the stillness of the streets in the
old French war-time, crying " Great news ! "
" Glorious news ! " when there were no news
at all.

The etymology of the cock mendacious is as
uncertain as that of the kingdom of Cockaigne.
Is the word derived from the " cock and pye " of
Justice Shallow—a thing said, but not the more
believed in ? Perhaps cock may have originated

in the patterer being frequently a coquin or rogue, or from the cock-and-bull story which Mr. Shandy's novel is ultimately settled to have been about. Or, does cock—a lie, a tale of news having no foundation whatever in fact, but still made public and persisted in—spring from the famous political hoax in which Lord *Coch*rane was said to have been implicated : the scandalous cock which for stockjobbing purposes, in the year eighteen hundred and fourteen, gave out Bonaparte to have been torn to pieces by Cossacks, and which had such disastrous consequences for one of the bravest officers of the British navy ?

This last theory, although sufficiently vraisemblable, is militated against by the indubitable existence of these chanticleers long anterior to Lord Cochrane's time. Their antiquity is highly respectable. Butler, who has something to say about almost every subject within the compass of human knowledge, has a wondrous appreciation of them in substance, if not in name. Listen to what he says in Hudibras, apropos of Fame :—

" There is a tall, long-sided dame,
(But wondrous light) yclcped Fame,
That like a thin chameleon boards
Herself on air, and eats her words;
Upon her shoulders wings she wears
Like hanging sleeves, lin'd through with ears,
And eyes, and tongues, as poets list,
Made good by deep mythologist.
With these she through the welkin flies,
And sometimes carries truth, oft lies;
With letters hung, like Eastern pigeons,
And Mercuries of furthest regions;
Diurnals writ for regulation
Of lying, to inform the nation,
And by their public use to bring down
The rate of whetstones in the kingdom.
About her neck a packet mail,
Fraught with advice, some fresh, some stale;
Of men that walk'd when they were dead,
And cows of monsters brought to bed;
Of hailstones big as pullet's eggs,
And puppies whelp'd with twice two legs;
A blazing star seen in the west
By six or seven men at least..

This quotation brings me to a topic which I have
been meditating upon from the commencement of
this article, and without which it would be singu-
larly incomplete: I mean newspaper chanticleers.
In snug little corners of that British Press, of
which we are all so justly proud and jealous,

eccentric gallinaceous figments nestle, crow, and clap their wings exceedingly. They are periodical in their appearance. Long debates, interesting news from abroad, great exhibitions, religious uproars, violent controversies as to whether Biffin calling Miffin a rascal meant therein anything to the prejudice of Wiffin; who, as a rascal, would be of course and for ever compromised in the opinion of both Chiffin and Piffin: these will occasionally drive bright chanticleer out of the columns of the London newspaper, and compel him to betake himself to those of the provincial journal. He will crow harmlessly till the metropolitan public begin to be satiated with the realities of authentic news; till the Episcopalians and Dissenters, magnanimously forgetting their former differences, combine heart and hand to fall foul of the Bhuddists; till Biffin assures Miffin that he never considered him a rascal at all, but rather as something nearly approximating to an angel. Then, and especially in the piping times of peace and profound tranquillity, doth chanticleer move modestly London-ward again.

Let me see if I cannot enumerate a few favourite newspaper chanticleers. I will not insult your understanding by allusion to the enormous gooseberries, singular freaks of nature, showers of frogs, cats found in gas-pipes, disco-veries of Roman remains, and human skeletons; which are the oldest, weakest, flimsiest known. They have passed into jokes long ago; and news-papers with even a shadow of modesty are ashamed to give insertion to them now. But there are others more insidious, less derisively scouted. There is the French war-steamer which hovers about the coast of Lincolnshire, some-where between Saltfleet and Great Grimsby; the officers of which are continually making sound-ings, or are landing to take sketches of the coast and adjacent scenery; all with an evident view to an approaching invasion, and to the infinite dismay of that great grandfather of lies, the oldest inhabitant; the plunging into newspaper

correspondence of our esteemed townsman, Mr.
Flubbers, who remembers the invasion panic of
eighteen hundred and four, and suggests that
now is the time for Government to purchase the
secret of the Flubbers' explosive sabre and the
Flubbers' asphyxiating (long range) syringe! and
the display of one hundred per cent. extra vigi-
lance by our active and experienced commander
of the coast-guard, Lieutenant Lopside. Dear
me! How many times that French war-steamer
has turned up. Off St. Michael's Mount in Corn-
wall; off the Orkneys and Shetland islands; off
Mull and Bute and Arran; off Galway, Brighton,
Torquay, and Beechey Head. She has always
been ready, at a newspaper pinch, off Dover.
The daily increasing intimacy and cordiality of
our relations with France, though, have brought
this belligerous vessel into some little disfavour;
and for it there have begun to be frequently substituted such anecdotes as—"There is now in the
possession of Mr. Spong of this town a double-
barrelled pistol of antique workmanship, pre-

sented to his ancestor Captain Hugh Spong by
Marshal Turenne, during the campaign of the
allied English and French armies in sixteen
hundred and fifty-six—seven." Or, " our readers
will be pleased to learn that it was the proud
privilege of our worthy host, Bootjohn, of the
Royal Leathers Hotel, to confer a considerable
obligation upon the present ruler of the French
nation some years since. The illustrious personage who was then staying at the Royal
Leathers, being in temporary difficulties, Bootjohn not only forgave him the amount of his
score, but also, and without the least hope of
return, lent him one and ninepence and a clean
shirt. We rejoice to learn that the whole amount
has been most honourably repaid by H—s I—p—l
M—j—y: the remittance being accompanied by a
highly flattering autograph letter from N—p—n
the Third."

There was some half-dozen years ago a highly
favourite little chanticleer crowing most lustily,
and attributing English, Scotch, or Irish extrac-

tion, and even existing relatives, to the imperial family of France, their generals, courtiers, and dependents. Thus, we used to be informed (Slugborough Herald) that the Empress's maternal uncle is now residing as a cheese and bacon factor at Epidermisnock, Argyleshire. It may be interesting to know (Foggington Courier) that the present Emperor of F——e was clandestinely married in eighteen hundred and thirty-six to Miss Chilian Pickles of this town. The I—p—l bride died soon after the incarceration of her adventurous husband in the citadel of H—m; but four children, the offspring of the marriage, are yet alive, two of whom are receiving a brilliant though solid education at the establishment of the Misses W——, not a hundred miles from here.

Multitudes of other chanticleers there be, to which I can but barely allude. The gallant gay Lotharios who elope with the lady of a highly respected baronet, to the consternation of the county and the ultimate employment of the gentlemen of the long robe; the heartless monsters who marry four different young ladies at four different churches on the same day; the would-be Benedicks who advertise for a wife—a lady having a small independence—and are entrapped into correspondence with gentlemen writing disguised female hands, and make appointments and keep them, and are ultimately brought to great shame and ridicule; the faithless swains who leave their intended brides at the church-door, and bolt off to Australia; the brutes who eat two legs of mutton, half a dozen live rats, and a pound of candles, for a wager; the criminals who were hanged twenty years ago, and are now alive and universally respected in Lower Canada; the railway navvies who come into fortunes of fifty thousand pounds, and immediately go mad with joy; the gentleman wearing eight watch-chains, who is continually travelling up and down the London and North Western Railway; the stingy nobleman at a fashionable watering-place, whose wife is saved from drowning by an honest boatman,

and who recompenses the hardy son of Neptune
with twopence; the nonogenarian paupers whose
demise is recorded under the heading, " Death of
a character;" the cuckoos that sing so early and
the blackbirds that sing so late; the weather
which is so astonishingly mild, and the Swedish
turnips that have attained so extraordinary a size:
these are a few of the newspaper chanticleers.
They are, in a general way, harmless enough.
And if the country newspapers who pay that
Cochin-China chanticleer, " Our London Correspondent," for his weekly letter, find their account
in it, so be it. I never knew him to be right
about anything; but he *may be,* some day.

MADAME BUSQUE'S.

BELIEVE me, Eusebius (to be classical and genteel), that many more good things exist in this world than are dreamt of in any philosophy —from that of the most rose-coloured optimist to that of the sourest cynic. Don't put any faith in yonder ragged, morose, shameful old man, who, because he lives in a tub instead of decent lodgings, and neglects, through sulky laziness, to trim his hair and beard and wear clean body-linen, calls himself Diogenes and a philosopher, forsooth. If the old cynic would only take the trouble to clean the horn sides of his lantern, and trim the wick of the candle within it, he would not find it quite so difficult to find an honest man. That all is vanity here below, I am perfectly ready to admit; but have no confidence in the philosophy, which, with its parrot-prate of the Prince of Wisdom's apophthegm—vanity—turns up its nose at, or pretends to ignore, the existence of the hidden good. Believe me, good is everywhere.

Poor, naked, hungry, sick, wronged as we may be through long years, snug incomes, well-cut coats, good dinners, sound health, justice and fame will come, must come at last, if we will only wait, and hope, and work. All have not an equal share, and some men, by a continuous infelicity which the most submissive are tempted to regard as an adverse and remorseless fate, fall down weary and die upon the very threshold of mundane reward; but let any average man—the medium between Miserimus and Felicissimus— look retrospectively into himself, and consider how many good things have happened to him unexpectedly, unasked for, undeserved; how many happinesses of love, friendship, sight, feeling, have come upon him unawares—have "turned up," so to say familiarly. A great Italian poet has said, that there is no greater sorrow than the remembrance in misfortune of the happy time. It can be scarcely so. It is balm rather than anguish for a man when fortune has thrown the shadow of a cypress over him, to recall the dear friends, the joyous meetings, the good books, the leafy days of old; for with the remembrance comes hope that these good things (present circumstances looking ever so black) will return again. It is only when we know that we have spurned, misused, wasted the jewelled days in the year's rosary, that remembrance becomes sorrow; for Remembrance then is associated with Monsieur Remorse; and we wish—ah, how vainly! ah, how bitterly!—that those days had never been, or that they might be again, and we use them better.

All things, good or bad, are relative; and though it would not be decent to express as much joy for the discovery of a good dinner as of a good friend, yet, both being relatively good in their way, I may be permitted to rejoice relatively over both in my way. I have not been very successful lately in the friendship line; but in the article of dinners I have really made a discovery. A succulent daily banquet has popped upon me suddenly; and I feel bound to record its excellences here, to the glory of the doctrine of fortuitous good in general, and of Madame Busque in particular.

I am resident in Paris, and feel the necessity of dining seven consecutive times a week. Such a necessity is not felt in the same degree in London. A man may take a chop in the City, a snack at lunch time, a steak with his tea, a morsel after the play. None of these are really dinners, but are considered sufficient apologies for them. Moreover, you can call upon a friend, and be asked to take a "bit of dinner" with him. People don't ask you to take a bit of dinner with them in Paris. With the French, dinner is an institution. You are asked to it

solemnly.   Probably you dine at a restaurant,
and know how much the repast costs your friend;
for you see him pay the bill.   Besides, going out
to dinner costs more money in gloves, fine linen,
starch, cab-hire, and losses at cards afterwards,
than a first-rate dinner given by yourself to yourself.   So, as I am neither a diplomatist, a sub-
scriber to a table-d'-hôte, a marrying man, or a
pique-assiette (by which I mean an individual
who gets invited to grand dinners by asking to
be asked), I find that the great majority of my
quotidian dinners have to be provided at my own
cost and charges.   I cannot dine at home; in the
first place, because one can do scarcely anything
at home in France save sleep; in the second
place, because I am alone, and must have company at dinner, be it only a waiter, a chandelier,
or that bald-headed old gormandiser with the
legion of honour, full of gravy and gravity, who
sits opposite to me at the Café Corazza, eats
seven courses, and has two silver hooks fastened
to the lappels of his coat, whereon to suspend the

napkin that shields his greedy old shirtfront from falling sauces.

Now I like dining at the Café Corazza, which was kept, in my time, by Ouix my friend. I knew him when he was about ninety years old; rouged; had curly hair and moustaches as black as jet, and used to tell stories of the days when he was maître-d'hôtel to Charles the Tenth, and brought in the first dish, dressed—Ouix, not the dish—in a court suit and a sword by his side. I like all the down-stairs Palais Royal dinners; Verrey's; Vefour's; the Three Provençal Brothers. I like Vachette's on the Boulevard. I like the newly invented Dîners de Paris, where for three francs fifty you may eat like an alderman. I like the Blue Quadrant; the House of Gold; the restaurant of the Magdalen. I like chevets, lobsters, and delicacies out of season. I like Marengo fowls, eels as female sailors, ortolans, blown omelettes, pies of fat liver, truffled turkeys, and kidneys jumped with wine of Champagne. They are good, and I like them; so do wiser and better men. I like a bumper of Burgundy to be filled, filled for me, and to give to those who prefer it Champagne. I like Beaune, Mâcon, Chablis, Sauterne, Lafitte, Médoc, Thorius Chambertin, Pommard, Clos Vougeot, Romauée Mercury (not blue pill by any means), and all the generous wines of the Golden Coast which are so delicious and are growing so wofully dear. In a word, I like good dinners; but alas! my name is not Rothschild, nor Royalty, nor Matthew Marshall. I can dine well once in a way, and that is all.

Resident in Paris some time ago, I had dined well—very well, once, perhaps twice in a way: and began to recognise the necessity of mediocrity in dining. No more for me were the golden columniated down-stairs saloons of the Palais Royal. Gold and columns and plate glass I could have in the upper apartments of that palace of gastronomy, and at a very moderate price; but the good meats, good sauces, good wines—they remained below. "Prix fixé" stared me in the

face. Dinners at a fixed tariff of prices and a
fixed tariff of badness. I could have six courses
for one and eightpence, but what courses!
Gloom began to settle upon me. I saw visions
of dirty little restaurants in back streets; of
biftecks like gutta percha; of wine like pyro-
ligneous acid, with a dash of hemlock in it to give
it body; of sour bread in loaves of the length of
a beefeater's halberd; of winy stains on the table-
cloth; of a greasy waiter; of a pervading odour
of stale garlic; of having to ask the deaf man
with the asthma and the green shade over his
eyes yonder, for the salt. Better I said, to buy
cold halves of fowls at the roasters' shops, and
devour them in the solitude of my fifth floor;
better to take to a course of charcuterie or cold
pork-butchery; Lyons sausages, black puddings,
pigs' feet, polonies with garlic, or sparerib with
savoury jelly. Better almost to go back to the
Arcadian diet of red-shelled eggs, penn'orths of
fried potatoes, fromage de Brie, and ha'porths of
ready-cooked spinach—of which, entre nous, I had

had in my time some experience. I was meditating between this and the feasibility of cooking
a steak over a French wood fire at home (a feat
never yet accomplished, I believe, by mortal
Englishman); I had almost determined to sub-
scribe for a month to a boarding-house in the
Banlieue, where the nourishment, as described on
the public walls, was "simple but fortifying,"
when the genius of fortuitous good threw Madame
Busque in my way.

Through the intermediary of a friend, be it
understood. He and I had dined well, the once,
twice, or thrice in a way at which I have hinted.
He mentioned at the conclusion of our last repast
that he must really dine at Madame's to-morrow.

I don't know what time in the afternoon it
was, but it was getting very near dinner-time. A
certain inward clock of mine that never goes
wrong told me so unmistakeably. It was very
cold, but we were sitting outside a café on the
Boulevard; which you can do in Paris till the
thermometer is all sorts of degrees below zero.

We were sitting there of course merely for the purpose of reading the latest news from America; but in deference to received café opinion, we were imbibing two petits verres of absinthe, which is a delicious cordial of gall, wormwood, and a few essential oils, and which mixed with a little aniseed and diluted with iced water will give a man a famous appetite for dinner. And thereanent I ventured to propound the momentous question: " Where shall we dine ? "

" Well," said my friend, " I was thinking of— of a crib—well, a sort of club in fact, where I dine almost every day when I am in Paris."

I suggested that he might have some difficulty in introducing me, a stranger, to the club in question.

" Why, no," he answered; " because you see it isn't exactly a club, because it's a sort of 'creamery;' and, in fact, if you don't mind meeting a few fellows, I think we'd better dine there."

I suggested that we had better go home and dress.

"Oh," exclaimed my friend, "nobody dresses there. To tell the truth, it's only at Madame Busque's; and so I think we'd better be off as fast as we can, for nobody waits for anybody there."

I confided myself blindly to the guidance of my friend, consoling myself with the conviction that whatever the club or "creamery" might be, the dinner could be but a dinner after all, and amount to so many francs on this side a napoleon.

We went up and down a good many streets, whose names I shall not tell you; for, unless I know what sort of a man you be, and what are your likings and dislikings, I would not have you go promiscuously to Madame Busque's, and perchance abuse her cookery afterwards. At length, after pursuing the sinuosities of a very narrow street, one of the old, genuine, badly-paved, worse lighted streets of Paris, we slackened our footsteps before a lordly mansion,—a vast hotel, with a porte-cochère and many-barred green shutters.

My heart sank within me. This must be some dreadfully aristocratic club, I thought, and still mentally I counted my store of five-franc pieces, and wondered tremblingly whether they played lansquenet after dinner.

"Is it here?" I faltered.

"Not exactly," answered my companion, "but next door,—behold!"

He raised his hand and pointed to a little sign swinging fitfully in the night air and the light of a little lamp; and I read these words :—

"SPECIALITÉ DE PUMPKIN PIE."

"Enter," said my friend.

We entered a little, a very little shop, on whose tiny window-panes were emblazoned half-effaced legends in yellow paint, relative to eggs, milk, cream, coffee, and broth at all hours. A solitary candle cast a feeble light upon a little counter, where there was a tea-cup and an account-book of extreme narrowness, but of prodigious length. Behind the counter loomed in the darkness visible some shelves, with many bottles of many sizes. Some tall loaves were leaning up in a corner, as if they were tired of being the staff of life, and wanted to rest themselves. A spectre of a pumpkin, a commentary of the text outside, winked in the crepuscule like a yellow eye. There were no eggs, broth, cream, or coffee to be seen; but there was a pleasant odour of cooking palpable to the olfactory nerves, and this was all.

"Push on," said my friend.

I pushed on towards another little light in the distance, and then I became sensible of a stronger and yet pleasanter odour of cooking; of a cheery voice that welcomed my friend as Monsieur Tompkins (let us say), and of another calmer, softer, sweeter voice, that saluted him as her "amiable cabbage,"—both female voices, and good to hear.

Pushing still onwards, I found myself in a very small many-sided apartment, which, but for a round table and some chairs, seemed

furnished exclusively with bottles. There were
bottles here and bottles there, bottles above and
bottles below, bottles everywhere, like the water
round the ship of the Ancient Mariner; but the
similarity stopped there, for there were many
drops to drink. At the round table, more than
three parts covered with bottles, sat five men
with beards. They were all large in stature and
in beard, and were eating and drinking vigor-
ously. Pasted on the walls above were several
portraits in chalk, among which I immediately
recognised those of the five bearded guests.
Nobody spoke, but the five beards were bowed
in grave courtesy: the clatter of knives and
forks relaxed for a moment, to recommence
with redoubled ardour; and two additional
places were found for us at the round table with
miraculous silence and promptitude. Then the
proprietor of the cheery voice, a rosy-cheeked
country girl, with her handkerchief tied under
her chin, which at first suggested toothache, but
eventually became picturesque, placed before me

bread, butter, a snowy napkin, a knife and fork, and a bottle of wine. Then the calm, soft, sweet voice became a presence incarnated in a mild woman with a gray dress and sad eyes, who addressing me as " dear friend of Monsieur Tompkins," suggested potage,—in which suggestion I acquiesced immediately.

The round table was of simple oak, and there was no table-cloth. The chairs were straw-bottomed and exceedingly comfortable. The floor was tiled and sanded. A solitary but very large wax-candle burnt in an iron candlestick. The salt-cellar (to prevent any one asking or being asked for it) was neatly poised on the top of a decanter, and was visible to all. Pepper was a superfluity, so excellently seasoned were the dishes. At intervals hands appeared, very much in the White Cat fashion, and tendered sardines, olives, the mild cheese of Brie, the pungent Roquefort, and the porous Gruyère.

I don't mean to say that I had any ortolans, quails, forced asparagus, or hot-house grapes, at

Madame Busque's (though I might have had them too, by ordering them), but I do mean to declare, that I had as good, plentiful, clean, well-dressed a dinner as ever Brillat-Savarin or Dr. Kitchener would have desired to sit down to. Wines of the best, liqueurs of the best, coffee of the best, cigars of the best (these last at the exorbitant rate of a penny a piece), and, above all, conversation of the very best.

For you are not to suppose that the five bearded men were silent during the entire evening. Dinner once discussed, and cigars once lighted, it turned out that the proprietor of one beard was a natural philosopher; another an Oriental linguist; a third a newspaper correspondent; a fourth a physician; a fifth a vice-consul:—that all had travelled very nearly over Europe, had ascended Vesuvius, had smoked cigars in the Coliseum, had taken long walks in the Black Forest. Travel, anecdote, science, literature, art, political discussion, utterly free from personality or prejudice,—all these, with a good and cheap dinner, did I find haphazard at Madame Busque's.

Nor perhaps was this the only good thing connected with the "creamery." I have since found myself the only Englishman among sometimes not five, but fifteen subjects of a one time Great Republic, three thousand miles away; and up to this moment I have never heard the slightest allusion to guessing, calculation, gouging, bowie-knifeing, repudiation, lynching, loco-focos, know-nothings, "Hard-shells," alligators, snags, or sawyers, or any of the topics on which our Republican cousins are supposed almost exclusively to converse. More than this, the much-to-be-abhorred questions of dollars or cents are never broached by any chance.

I need not say that I dine very frequently at Madame Busque's. I like her; her cookery; her guests; her good-humoured servant Florence, and her Pumpkin Pie, for which she has a speci-ality, and the confection of which was taught her by the vice-consul. I am not going to tell you how cheap her dinners are, or where they are to be had, till I know more of you; but if you will send to this office certificates of your good temper and citizenship of the world, I don't mind communicating Madame Busque's address to you, in strict confidence.

A VISIT TO BEDLAM.

ONE very gloomy Saturday afternoon in October, a hansom cab bore the instant narrator from the London-bridge terminus of the South Coast Railway, to the portals of Bethlehem Hospital. At Brighton an hour and a half before, I had left beautiful autumn weather; graceful Amazons curveting along the cliffs, pretty little amber-haired children paddling with their tiny toy-spades among the sand and shingle, or staring at the porcelain acrobats and india-rubber balloons in Mr. Chassereau's shop. Between. this Fairy land and Babylon the Great were but a roar and a rattle, a few tunnels and thirteen shillings to pay. Then the fog took possession of the train and its inmates. Then came shimmering in pellicles almost visible on the brumous bosom, the raw rime that rusts beards and moustaches; and we felt in all its inflexibility the grim, uncompromising, marrow-chilling, mind-depressing London October weather. A fit day, indeed, for a visit to Bethlehem.

We stood (I had a companion) before the great iron entrance-gates and looked on to a vast smooth lawn, of which the close shavenness offered some fantastic analogy, to my mind, of a rigidly-cropped madman's head. The grim perspective ended with that sweeping façade and stately cupola familiar as to its exterior to most London-bred men, but the secret of whose interior is as unknown to the majority of dwellers in the great city as the inside of Temple Bar or the White Tower. Many a time, as a child, have I wondered whether they kept the mad folks in that lofty dome—they making the roof ring with their shrieks. Not, therefore, was it without an indefinite feeling of perturbation that I

awaited the response to our summons on the gate-
bell. An answer soon came, however; and a
comely matron admitted us to the precincts of
London's oldest and most important lunatic
asylum. We were permitted to pass along the
gravelled walk skirting the lawn, and anon found
ourselves beneath the peristyle of the hospital.
The entrance-hall and staircase are of noble proportions, and remind one far more of the vesti-
bule of a West-end club than of the lobby of a
mad-house. In vain, too, did I look for Cibber's
famous statues; but my companion informed me
that as a last vestige of the dark, coercive Bedlam
days, they had been banished the hospital, and
removed, as mere relics, to the South Kensington
Museum. In their stead, I saw on the staircase
a vigorous though unfinished painting of "The
Good Samaritan" by an afflicted artist who has
been for years a patient on the "Government
side" of the hospital.

Pending the arrival of Doctor Hood, the skilful
and benevolent physician to Bethlehem Hospital,

to whom we were accredited, and to whom we
had sent our cards, we were ushered into a
spacious apartment overlooking the lawn, and
serving as a board-room for the governors of the
institution. Over the chimney there is a geome-
trical-looking portrait—I should say a Holbein,
or an excellent copy from that master, of the
eighth Harry. Then there is a portrait of Sir
Peter Laurie. Sir Peter was the beloved president
of the hospital; and all round the walls are the
armorial bearings blazoned on convex bosses,
with frames elaborately carved and gilt, of the
several presidents of the Royal hospitals, from
the Tudor's times to those of our gracious Lady
Queen Victoria. But we have still some little
time to wait, and there cannot be a better time
than this, I think, to interpolate a few remarks
bearing on the historical antecedents and actual
organisation of this remarkable charity.

Simon Fitz-Mary, sheriff, gave A.D. 1246,
certain lands in St. Botolph-without-Bishopsgate,
for the foundation of a priory of canons, brethren,

and sisters of the order of the Star of Bethlehem. Simon the founder's lands were on the spot afterwards known as old Bedlam, now Liverpool Street, Moorfields. It is described as an hospital, and was taken under the protection of the City in 1546, and in the same year Harry of the six wives, having in vain endeavoured to sell the freeholds of the lands and tenements to the Corporation, made a virtue of necessity and gave them in " frankalmaigne "—a free gift for ever. Hence I presume the obese benefactor over the marble mantel in Bethlehem's council chamber. The hospital had been an asylum for lunatics since 1402.

These Hospital Priory buildings escaped the Great Fire, but becoming dilapidated, were in 1675-6 demolished, and a new Bedlam built on ground (leased by the governors of the Corporation) on the south side of Moorfields. It was somewhat of a grand affair, architecturally; was designed by Robert Hook, and cost £17,000. The posterns of Hook's Bedlam gates were sur-

mounted by those stone figures sculptured by
Gabriel Cibber, of which I have already spoken.
In George the Second's time two additional
wings for incurable patients were erected. The
average number of inmates was 150, and the
hospital is described as consisting chiefly of two
immense galleries, one above the other, divided
in the centre by two iron gates—the male patients
on one side, the females on the other. There
were also some out-patients or pensioners, de-
mented, but not raving, and known as "Tom o'
Bedlams," who wore metal plates on their arms,
and were suffered to wander about the streets and
beg. Furthermore, to the shame of the eighteenth century, be it confessed that Bedlam Hospital was, till the year 1770, one of the lions
of London. The public were admitted for a
wretched fee, which yet brought in a considerable
revenue, to see the madmen "all alive," just as
they were enabled to see the wild beasts in
Exeter Change, or, as a few years before, the
bucks and men about town used to make up

parties of pleasure to see the women flogged in the court-room at Bridewell.*

In 1799 the hospital (which had been built on the shifting rubbish of the City Ditch, and in the short space of sixteen months) was reported to be desperately unsafe. It tottered on, however, till 1810, when the site was exchanged for eleven acres in St. George's-fields; the first stone of the present building was laid in 1812, and new Bedlam was completed in 1815. Two wings, for which the Government contributed £25,144, were built for the criminal lunatics, of whom the governors of the charity have the unwelcome charge. More new buildings and the dome were added between 1838 and 1845; and the present structure is three storeys high, and 897 feet in length. The dome is 150 feet in height from the ground. The improved system of management

---

* Not alone to us has the scandal attached of exhibiting madmen as a sight and show. It was with a party of Court dames that the Marquis of Worcester visited the Paris Bicêtre, and saw Salomon de Caux there; and so late as 1832, Mr. N. P. Willis was enabled for a few paras to see the caged maniacs in the madhouse of Constantinople.

was introduced in 1816; the system, indeed, mainly inaugurated at the Bicêtre and Charenton during the First Empire, by the benevolent Pinel. The new system of management did not come in before it was needed. The treatment of the insane up to the period named had been almost incredibly disgraceful. A narrative, even in outline, of the atrocities daily and hourly committed on the helpless patients in the Hospitals of Bedlam and St. Luke—outrages only surpassed, if surpassed they could be, by those wreaked on the miserable wretches confined in private asylums— would pollute this page. It is consoling to know that this new building in St. George's-fields has never been the scene of horrors similar to those recorded in the dismal and obsolete blue-book I speak of. I am glad to quit the ugly theme, to find myself once more in the board-room, with its evidence of the present, its furniture of the past, and this time with Doctor Hood at our elbow, and ready, not to gratify an idle curiosity, but to assist me in the performance of a steady and serious task. Quidnuncs and sightseers are by no means welcome as visitors to this abode of the saddest sorrow with which the Almighty, in his mysterious wisdom, has visited his creatures. The visitors admitted to inspect the establishment, by favour of the governor, treasurer, president, or physician, or by order from the Secretary of State, rarely exceed a yearly average of five hundred, and a large proportion of these consist of distinguished foreigners, statesmen, scientific men, and the like. There must be, indeed, something very worthy of inspection, and much from which hints may be taken, in the present condition of Bethlehem; for the uncompromising statistics of the Registrar-General tell us that here the average mortality is seven per cent. In other asylums the patients die at from thirteen to seventy-two per cent.

It is to be borne in mind, that Bethlehem is not strictly a pauper-lunatic asylum. The inmates are either criminal or unfortunate; the objects of a special care or of a special mercy: and while the slightest evincement of a wish for healthful employment is cheerfully met by the authorities, there does not seem to exist that feverish desire to utilise the patients—to make them "worth their salt," as it were, which is painfully palpable in some county institutions. In Bethlehem, those who are able and willing, are supplied with light and pleasant occupation about the house. A patient whose terrible attempt twenty years since all the world has heard, is the cleverest painter and grainer in the whole establishment, and a general "handy man;" but no attempt is made to force the inclinations of the patients, or to set them irksome tasks; and a sedulous, though to them invisible, supervision takes place, to avert the occurrence of accidents from the dangerous tools and implements they may use while working at their trades or in the gardens.

I purpose describing the female before the male gallery, as it is in many respects more interesting,

and exhibits in a more remarkable degree the
benefits derived from the absence of coercion,
and the substitution of amusements and light
enjoyments for a dull and rigorous restraint.
The first female ward I visited was occupied
principally by patients who were approaching con-
valescence, and it was easy to discern an *approach*
towards sanity, not only in the elegance and
cheerfulness of the decorations, but also in the
recreations and the occupations of the denizens
of the place. There is nothing absolutely repulsive in the rooms devoted to the most refractory
patients; but there is a marked and indispensable difference between their abode and the
gallery of which I am now speaking.

The long vista is crowded—though not in-
conveniently—with little trifles and knick-knacks
of comfort and refinement. Flowers, artificial
or natural, are to be found on every table.
Further ornamentation has been resorted to in
the way of climbing and trailing plants, and
in the interval between each window is either

a bust, or a print neatly framed and glazed, or
a cage containing a singing-bird. The quantity
of handsome busts and engravings distributed
through the whole of the wards is as surprising
as their presence is satisfactory. The engravings
are the gift of the late Mr. Graves, the eminent
publisher of Pall Mall. The authorities of Bethlehem Hospital cannot be too highly commended
for this introduction of an artistic element that
mitigates and well nigh nullifies the depressing
influences of the place. The very whitewash
necessary for health and cleanliness is tempered
to a cheerful hue, and picked out here and there
by streaks of red or blue. Verily, this was the
last place where I should have expected to have
seen in beneficial operation the prismatic canons
of Mr. Owen Jones. In the centre of the gallery wall there is a complete aviary full of joy-
ously-carolling birds; and these little songsters
seem to possess much power in raising the sometimes drooping spirits and soothing the troubled
minds of the unhappy persons who dwell here.

Heaven knows to what green fields, what spark-
ling streams, what chequered shades of brake
and thicket, the silver notes of the birds take
back their poor wool-gathering minds! Heaven
knows what dim and confused memories—re-
miniscences without a beginning or an end, or
perchance with a middle and no commencement or termination—are awakened by the sight
of these pictures and birds!

From the side facing the line of windows,
lead at intervals the sleeping apartments. The
doors of these rooms are kept locked during the
day, in order that the patients may not be for one
moment exempt from the kind and sisterly vigi-
lance of the attendants.

One figure of which we caught sight advanc-
ing along the female gallery requires a few words
at our hands. She is a patient, and is has-
tening to the dining-room, bearing some little
delicacy of extra diet which has been ordered by
the physician for one of her companions.

At a glance the spectator is impressed with the

hurried and pre-occupied object which character-
ises her, and with the anxious and almost agonised
expression which pervades her countenance. This
poor young woman labours under the impression
that she is approaching the table of the Lord,
that she will be too late, and that in consequence
her soul will be lost. Whenever she sees the
physician, or a stranger, she assails him with
questions and entreaties, all bewildered and semi-
incoherent, but all bearing on that awful errand
and that dreadful doubt. Of every figure in this
varied scene some strange characteristic trait
might be given, some stranger anecdote re-
lated; but I am bidden to forbear. Let me
hint, however, that the majority of the females
have been either governesses or maid-servants.
Over-study with the former, religion—or rather
religious hysteria and love—with the latter, have
been the proximate causes of their malady. Seven
years since the galleries of Bethlehem presented
a very different appearance to that which they
now do. There was kindness, and there were

comforts and necessaries; but there were none of those little luxuries and elegancies which are now so conspicuous and so beneficial in their influence.

In this particular gallery, now so prettily painted, so well carpeted, cheerfully lighted, and enlivened with prints and busts, with aviaries and pet animals, the walls were simply whitewashed; the furniture was meagre; the windows were so highly pitched that the patient had only the dreary look-out of the London sky. In those days there were no cheerful stoves nor ornamented chimney-pieces, and the sleeping apartments were lighted only by small circular *lucarnes* high above the reach of the occupant. In fact, that which was once a prison-cell has now become a cheery domestic room. The sleeping apartment of a docile female patient is furnished with a neat little bedstead with snowy drapery, a toilet-glass, a dressing-table, a cushioned easy-chair, and often much pretty decoration in the way of needlework d'oyleys and anti-macassars. The reader will doubtless and with some astonishment contrast the description of Bethlehem with the accounts he has been accustomed to listen to.

The changes for the better in Bethlehem Hospital within the last seven years have been truly marvellous. One excellent and amiable man deserves much praise for the social revolution within the walls of this whilom mansion of misery. To the liberality of the Governors, with Sir Peter Lauric and Mr. J. S. Johnson at their head, and the energy of Doctor Charles Hood, must be ascribed the admirable and highly useful improvements that have taken place. To his artistic taste the patients owe the innocent ornamentation of their former gloomy abode, which is now to them a source of solace and delight; and since the advent to the position of physician residentiary of Doctor Hood, this kind and wise labourer in the field of mercy has, together with his skilful and indefatigable assistant Doctor Helps, done

more to alleviate not only the physical pangs, but
the mental woes, of the afflicted beings under his
charge, than has perhaps been effected by any
medical practitioner in any asylum for the insane
throughout the country. Dogmatism and fana-
ticism are alike out of place in Bethlehem. Sua-
vity, cheerfulness, patience, good-humour, are the
best doctors. The patients, with all their comforts, luxuries, and amusements, by the very fact
of their tremendous and awful deprivation, are
already and must be miserable. The waters of
Lethe flow over the head of Idiocy, but not of
Insanity. Save only when in an access of frenzy,
I believe that all mad people are conscious of, and
possessed by, a sense of the unutterable wretched-
ness of their lot—of their doom to seek and
search for continually that which, God help them!
they seldom find on this side the grave—their
wits. It is a characteristic of the sage and patient
polity that now reigns in Bethlehem, that while
there is a chapel and a good and pious chaplain,
and while the consolations of religion are always

at their command, they are never teased with religion, they are never worried with misplaced sermons.

The reward of Doctor Hood is pleasurably manifest to every visitor that passes through the walls of Bethlehem. You see it in the patients who throng round the kind physician, to press his hand, to ask his advice, and whisper —Heaven knows what rambling nonsense sometimes—in his ear. Even the paralytic and bedridden nod and smile as the doctor passes— not with a vacant leer, but with a grateful meaning.

Scattered and scanty as are their poor senses, they know that the doctor is their friend; that he comes not with gags and fetters and scourges, but with tidings of help and comfort; that he comes to soothe and heal; and we all know that he is on his Master's business, that he is doing that which shall be done to him on the great day of reckoning; yea! a thousandfold and a millionfold of talents of imperishable gold and

silver for every twopence which the good Samaritan left at the inn for the wounded man who
had gone down to Jericho and fallen among
thieves.

It is no easy and no immediately thankful
task for a man of education and refinement to
abandon his beloved pursuits, the intercourse
of society, the comforts of home, and the relax-
ations of literature almost, and devote himself
to the perpetual perambulation of this *via dolo-
rosa*—for ever pacing up and down these cor-
ridors, unlocking wickets with his master-key,
and doomed to be called up at any hour of the
night, to have his ears filled from noon to night
with whimperings and croonings, with moans
and hysteric laughter. How he must cling to
a strange face, shipwrecked as he is in this
ocean of vacuous countenances! We see such
men as Dr. Hood and Dr. Helps patiently,
cheerfully resigning themselves to follow this
thorny path. We know that they have many
brethren in their calling—scholars, gentlemen,

philanthropists—equally patient, cheerfully laborious in the good work; and it is a reassuring and ennobling thing to know that vacancies among these knights of the order of mercy are always filled up—that there are always men ready and willing to take up their cross and follow the behests of Him who wept for our sufferings and suffered for us all.

It would be unjust in this case to omit a cordially favourable mention of the male and female attendants at Bethlehem Hospital. None of the cynical sternness of the hired nurse can be imputed to them. They do their spiriting very gently, and use their patients, not as though they were repulsive burdens, but in a brotherly and sisterly fashion. Some of these attendants have been in the asylum for twenty-two years, during which time not one accusation of misconduct has been alleged against them.

The onerous nature of their duties may be imagined, when we reflect that lunatic patients are often as feeble, as helpless, as exigent and perverse and fractious as children.

When Dr. Hood pays one of his cheerful visits to the ladies' work-room—fitted up with exquisite taste, and where convalescent and docile patients amuse or employ themselves in embroidery, fancy work, and flower-painting in water-colours—it is by no means an uncommon occurrence for him to be asked by one of the inmates for permission to go out "for a day's pleasure." Think not this is one of the vain and hopeless requests preferred by the maniac pining in his dismal captivity. If the patient be "well enough" permission is readily granted; and the Soho Bazaar, the Pantheon, or friends and relatives, are visited. I confess that few things surprised me more during my sojourn in this remarkable institution, than the calm intimation that there was scarcely a place of amusement in the metropolis to which Dr. Hood had not sent his patients, and that the great majority of them had participated in this privilege. To which I must add a more noteworthy postscript, that on no occasion has the physician had to regret the extension of such an indulgence.

The male gallery is of the same dimensions as the principal gallery, and is fitted up in a style similar, but not exactly identical, to that employed on the female side. There are fewer flowers and similar elegancies, but the comforts are the same, and there is the same fondness manifested for pet birds and animals, cats, canaries, squirrels, &c. The patients amuse themselves with games of bagatelle, cards, painting, reading, &c. In one corner of the apartment is a party playing chess; others are killing time with music, or with that great consolator the tobacco-pipe. Still, many of the patients take no pleasure in any kind of amusement, but for hours will sit or stand alone, wrapped in thought, some in the attitude of listening, some with sunken heads and hands clasped behind them, others with

their arms pinned to their sides like recruits
in the presence of the drill-sergeant. Others
pace the long gallery incessantly, pouring out
their woes to those who would listen to them,
or if there be none to listen, to the dogs and
cats, or just as frequently to the air.

The Long Gallery gives access to a very excellent library. The leading journals and periodicals
of the day are to be found on the tables, and on
the bookshelves is a capital collection of the
standard works of modern literature. The library
is always well frequented. Many of the patients
are well educated and accomplished men; more
than one have been celebrated in intellectual
pursuits. I need not remind those that are
familiar with asylum interiors, that one may be
for a long period in conversation with a lunatic
who will in all respects behave as a rational being
till you touch on the subject of his delusion.
Pursuing the plan I proposed to myself at the
commencement, I will not particularise the hallu-
cinations that came under my notice. This is no

journal of psychological medicine; and to make the special delusions of a madman a topic for picturesque essay-writing is only pandering to a morbid curiosity. Of course, there are kings and emperors and pontiffs among the patients. So there have been, I dare say, for centuries, and so there are in every mad-house in the world. As a fact very important as evidence in favour of a system not only of non-coercion, but of positive indulgence, let it be recorded that books or periodicals being wantonly torn or defaced are unknown in the institution. It would seem that the mad folks are wiser in their generation than the human monkeys roving at large who tear and smear periodicals, or who, the scandal of this age, have been lately outraging books and maps in the reading-room of the British Museum.

With a brief allusion to two remaining and most noticeable features of the "new system" of management, my brief survey of Bethlehem Hospital must be brought to a conclusion. The two corresponding saloons at the extremity of the wings, and which are of spacious dimensions, and lighted by large louvre windows, contain, the one a billiard-room, much frequented by the male patients in the evening; the other, a ball-room. The latter is on the female side, and during the autumn and winter months balls are constantly given to the inmates, both male and female, who appear thoroughly to appreciate the enjoyment provided for them. Both Doctor Hood and Doctor Helps join the patients at these entertainments. Refreshments, consisting of home-made wines, and ale, cake, biscuit, and fruit, are handed down at intervals. Many of the patients remain seated the whole evening, silent, moody, and abstracted, taking no interest in the excitement of the dance. At eleven o'clock, "God save the Queen" is sung, and the poor creatures go to bed —the majority amused and pleased.

I have said that the more docile often see the outside world, and mingle in the recreations of the people who are not quite mad enough to be received into Bethlehem—I mean yourself, myself, and the rest of the ladies and gentlemen who are so conceited about their sanity. In wet weather, the vast extent of the galleries affords no mean opportunity for exercise. For fine weather, there are spacious and well laid-out gardens, with lawns and parterres, at the rear of the edifice; in which gardens, under the care of the attendants, some patients take exercise, some smoke, some run and leap, some stand immovable for hours, gazing at the sky, the shrubs, or the ground. No patient looks at his neighbour. But neither passionists nor quietists ever do the slightest injury to the trees, or shrubs, or flowers.

The last of the doors was unlocked, and my tour was at an end. We went back to Doctor Hood's study, and I looked through an album of photographs taken from patients in their accesses of mania, and in their lucid moments. I glanced at reports and balance-sheets, and learned that the hospital, though not plethoric with wealth, enjoyed an adequate revenue, administered with a

wise liberality and discretion. I learned that the
improvements were carried out at a great cost;
and I thought that he who would grudge one penny
of a sum, however liberal, towards such a merciful
purpose must be a crooked-hearted curmudgeon,
only fit to farm pauper children, and make a
profit out of them.

I left Bethlehem Hospital with the conviction
that it was the noblest, and yet the least preten-
tious, of England's many noble but often osten-
tatious charities. I came out in the October
world, and found it as cold, and foggy, and
muddy as usual. I dined, and went to the play
and the club; but I had dreamt of Bethlehem,
sleeping and waking, for days. I mused on what
I had seen; I was haunted by what I had heard.
I thought of the luxuries and comforts, the plants
and the pet animals, the books and the periodicals, the billiard and the ball-room, the skill and
tenderness of the physician; but all these, to my
mind, would not fill up the vast abyss of human
mental misery yawning beneath the lofty dome in

St. George's-fields; and, with an inward groan, I murmured, "Let me be crippled, deaf, blind, paralytic, mutilated, even to negation of outward form, if such be Thy will, but not mad, O Lord, not mad!"

SIR JOHN BARLEYCORN AT HOME.

"How long, O scribe!" I expect to hear an indignant public in a Catilinian manner exclaim, when the subject-matter of this article is palpable to its gaze—"how long, O writer, is our propriety to be offended, our sensibility shocked, our gentility disregarded, by your irreverent and incorrigible recurrence to the vulgar subject of beer? Have you no shame, no reticence, no sense of decorum, no respect for your superiors? If you had lived a hundred years ago and in Grub Street, you would have starved; unless, indeed, you had secured the friendship of Mr. Thrale. If you were a Chinese literato, His Celestiality would bamboo you to death; if you had been one of Tippoo Saib's moonshees, he would have decapitated you; one of Sultan Mahmoud's poets, you would have been bowstrung. Be grateful, then, that you live in the nineteenth century, under the merciful dispensation of wise and humane laws and increasing civilisation. Be thankful for the leniency which renders your immediate incarceration and deportation beyond sea illegal; and for that sagacious discretionary power placed in the hands (and eyes) of all classes of readers who, if they do not like your subject matter, need not read what you write."

In sooth I am almost ashamed, and am reluctant, and hang back, and blush—if one can blush in pen and ink—now that (a portion of my task being accomplished and the houses and drinkers for a time disposed of) it becomes my bounden duty to treat of beer itself. So I am fain to take heart, and gird up my loins to the task, catching at, nervously, an additional, though fragile, consolation, that my subject is at least not a dry one.

It is my present purpose to relate to you the particulars of a visit which I once paid to a very worthy knight, a friend of mine, whose family has enjoyed great fame and consideration in the English country for upwards of five hundred years— Sir John Barleycorn.

This knight, though he has never aspired to any grade superior to that which his equestrian spurs confer on him, has been time out of mind the boon companion of emperors and monarchs; yet, with a wise magnanimity, he hath not, at the same time, disdained to enliven the leisure moments of clowns and churls—yea, down even unto vagrants and Abraham-men. One of Sir John's panegyrists sings—

" The Beggar who begges
Without any legges,
And scarcely a rag on his bodye to veile,
Talks of princes and kynges
And all these fine thynges,
When once he has hold of a tankard of ale."

Ale being, indeed, the article for the confection of which, and his many convivial qualities, Sir

John hath, in times both ancient and modern, been principally celebrated. So highly esteemed was his ale of old, that another poetic eulogiser of our knight, in reverent station no less than a bishop, hath declared—as we previously set forth —his willingness that both his outward back and side should " go bare, go bare," provided that his inner man were irrigated with a sufficiency of "jolly good ale and old." And in our own days there have not been wanting bards enthusiastic in sounding the praises of Sir John Barleycorn and his ale, from him that writ the affectionate strophe commencing with " Oh, brown beer, thou art my darling," to that other lapwing of Parnassus, the democratic admirer of Sir John, who, in his lay, calls down fierce maledictions on those who would attempt "to rob a poor man of his beer."

It was with an honest pride that Sir John (a burly, red-faced, honest-looking country gentleman, in a full suit of brown and silver, with a wig of delightful whiteness) discoursed to me of these matters, when last stopping in town, at the coffee-house where he entertained me. "Yes," he said, "I and my ancestors have seen fine days, I can tell you. We have entertained more kings, crowned and discrowned, than Monsieur Voltaire's Candide ever saw supping together at the Carnival of Venice. My father was a favourite (and rivalled it sharply with Prince Potemkin too) with Catherine of Russia. The Polish nobles delighted in him, and the Muscovite Boyards literally drank up his words. Nor was he less considered here in England. Queen Bess honoured my great-grandfather; and it was with a foaming tankard of my great-uncle's October brew that the serving-man soused Sir Walter Raleigh when, surprising him smoking a pipe of tobacco, he, the servitor, thought his master to be a-fire. Down where I dwell the monks of the old abbey frequently chose their cellarer for abbot, so high a respect had they for even those remotely connected with the Barleycorns. But we have seen in our time evil days. We have been vilified, scandalised, made responsible for all the evils which an indiscriminate and immoderate use of our good gifts may bring upon intemperate persons. The last Sir John was indicted and tried for his life at Glasgow by a temperance poet; and had he not put himself upon his country and proved beyond a doubt that none of the genuine Barleycorns ever meant harm to the people of Scotland; but that it was an idle intemperate, deboshed fellow, smelling terribly of peat smoke—one Usquebagh, who had formed an illicit alliance with a cast-off hussey of the Malt family—that had through them endeavoured to bring the Barleycorns to shame; had he not done this it would have gone hard with him. You may see the report of the case now in a Scotch poem, called The Trial of Sir John Barleycorn. I myself, as harmless a man (though I say it) as ever broke bread, have been treated in these latter days as something very little better than a murderer, a male Brinvilliers, and my ale as a sort of *aqua tofana.* 'Twas a French chemist did me this turn, thinking to annihilate me. You shall take coach with me to-morrow, and we will go to my ancestral seat, where the principal branch of our family hath had their habitat since Harry the Eighth's time. Sir, you shall do John Barleycorn the honour of a visit at his poor house at Burton-on-Trent."

Whereupon this jovial knight (he should be a baronet, for his title is hereditary, but he stoutly disclaims the bloody hand, and writes himself simple *eques*) called for t'other flaggon; which, being discussed, he paid the reckoning, and appointing a rendezvous for the morrow, swaggered off to bed, humming Bishop Still's old air. 'Tis said he sleeps in a beer-barrel, and washes himself in the morning by turning the tap of a full cask of Burton ale over his face and hands : but that is no business of mine.

"Burton-on-Trent," Sir John vouchsafed to tell me, whiling away the time, as we rolled along the London and North-Western Railway, Birmingham-ward, " has been celebrated for beer

and breweries for many hundred years. Old
Doctor Plot, in his Staffordshire Natural History,
mentions the celebrity of Burton-on-Trent for
malting. The great Parliamentary general, my
Lord Essex (a worthy nobleman, but on the
wrong side), writing in sixteen hundred and
forty-four on the subject of a garrison to be
placed in Burton, says that the inhabitants were
'chiefly clothiers and maltsters.' Sir Walter
Scott alludes to Burton and its brewers, in Ivan-
hoe.   Sir Oswald Mosely, in his History of
Tutbury Castle, tells us that the intelligence of
the Babington conspiracy was conveyed to Queen
Mary Stuart, while a prisoner in Tutbury Castle,
by a brewer at Burton. Who knows but that
the Scots queen may have been kept in knowledge of the progress of the plot for her
deliverance by treasonable documents wrapped
round the bungs of the ale-casks? Doctor Shaw
adverts to the Burton breweries as famous and
flourishing in seventeen hundred and twenty;
and the records of our house show that the

founder of that branch thereof, now managed by two well-known firms, was in extensive commercial communication with Russia, Poland, and the Danubian provinces—all great consumers of the sweet strong ale of Burton—early in the reign of George the Second. Yet, in England," resumed Sir John, taking breath, and murmuring something against confounded railways and in favour of a cool tankard, "the celebrity of the Burton beers was almost purely local till within late years. The Burton Barleycorns sent but little of their wares to London. The Peacock in Gray's Inn Lane is mentioned by Doctor Shaw (seventeen hundred and thirty-eight) as the first Burton-ale house. To be sure, there were in those days only packhorse roads to London. There are people alive now in Burton who can remember to have heard their mothers tell of the first construction of the roads to the neighbouring towns."

Swiftly the rapid steam-serpent bore us towards the home of beer; and my travelling companion told me long stories of the herculean labours of the brewers, whom he liked to consider as the Barleycorn intendants or stewards; how one of them and the Russian ministry fell in and fell out; and how he put his trust in princes, and was deceived accordingly.

"But respecting pale ale," I asked—"pale ale —bitter ale. The delight and solace of the Indian subaltern in his fuming bungalow; the worthy rival of brandy pawnee; the drink without which no tiffin can be complete, no journey by dawk possible: the favourite drink here in England of lord and bagman, duchess and nurse; the much admired tonic for invalids and persons of weak interiors?"

"I'll tell you. While in London in eighteen hundred and twenty-two, one of my brewers was dining with an East Indian director, and was talking with some despondency of his trade anxieties :—

"'Why don't you try the India Trade?' asked the director.

"'Don't know of it.'

"'Leave the cold countries: try the hot. Why not brew India beer?' The director rang the bell, and ordered his butler to bring a bottle of India Ale which had been to India and back. Sir John Barleycorn's representative tasted it. Went home. The director sent him a dozen of the beer by coach. The brewer took counsel with *his* head brewer, a practical hard-headed man, the hereditary maltster of the firm. They held a solemn council with locked doors, and the result was that the first mash of the East India Pale Ale, of which more than ten thousand hogsheads are now shipped off annually to the three presidencies, was brewed in a tea-pot.

"There, sir," concluded sir John. "That's the true legend of pale ale. Not so interesting, perchance, as the tradition concerning the discovery of roast pig in China, the invention of grog, or the first preparation of pickled herrings by the Dutch. There is nothing new under the sun, and there can be no doubt that bitter ale was well known to the ancient Hebrews, as the editor of Notes and Queries will tell you. But here's Tamworth."

We traversed a yard as thickly strewed with empty barrels as Woolwich dockyard is with empty cannons; but a peaceful arsenal—a field of drink and not of death. There were lounging or working about the yard sundry big draymen, selected, as draymen should be, for their size and strength; all possessing a curious family resemblance to their cousins-german the Barclay and Perkins, and Truman and Hanbury men in London. They were backing horses, and performing curious feats with drays, and toppling full casks about like gigantic ninepins, with such ease and such grave and immoveable countenances that I could not help thinking of the goblin players for whom Rip Van Winkle set up the pins that very long night on the Catskill Mountains; or of those other players whose skittle-ground was on the Hartz in Germany, and who had Frederic Barbarossa for their

president. We mounted a steep flight of stairs,
into a large apartment and watched the sacks
of malt being slowly hoisted up by a crane
through the window.

The malt is first weighed, then sifted in a
hopper with a double screen; then, being pre-
cipitated up a curious contrivance called a
"Jacob's Ladder," is crushed between a series
of rollers like a dredging machine. And by
"crushing," Sir John took particular care to
inform me, he did not mean "smashing." The
corporeal integrity of the barleycorn is preserved,
not intact, but by being with its germinatory
offshoots "starred," turned inside out, as it were,
but still collapsible to its original dimensions.
Crushed, this malt passes into a long trough,
and is pushed by an Archimedian screw from
hopper to hopper (each lined with zinc, and looking like a floury Erebus), amidst clouds of
minute farinaceous particles which got down my
throat and into my eyes, and set me sneezing
and coughing uproariously. These different hop-

pers come down into, and are all feeders of the
great mash-tub in the room below. I descended
a staircase into this mashing hall; and as soon
as my eyes (scarcely quit yet from the floury
simoom) had recovered from the blinding and
scalding effects of the clouds of steam, I gazed
around. Vessels resembling washing-tubs on a
Megatherian scale met my eyes on all sides.
These tubs are mash-tubs, each of which will
hold one hundred quarters of malt; each large
copper has a capacity for three hundred and
seventy barrels; and in them the malt (supplied from the hoppers above) is mashed into
a gruel thick and slab—the hot water being first
let in—mashed by huge sails or paddles working with a circular motion, with huge velocity,
yet capable of being stopped in a moment,—until
the starchy matter in the malt is, by heat and
moisture and motion, converted into wort—the
wort we have been all so familiar with in our
young days when home-brewing took place; and
for furtively consuming which (hot, sweet, and weak)

from half-pint mugs, our youthful ears have been frequently boxed. There is one monster tub here, Sir John told me, whose feeder will be put in requisition to supply three thousand barrels or ninety-six thousand gallons of ale, the amount of one single order. I remark here, on the authority of the Barleycorn knight, that " light beers " do not require a " stiff mash; " that every hundred quarters of malt take upon an average seven hours-and-a-half mashing; and that in the brewery we are now surveying there can be mashed in the Barleycorn interest as much as fifteen hundred quarters a week. The several minor details, relative to the exact proportions of water, temperature, and other niceties would not, I opine, be in any way interesting to the general reader; there are besides slight points of trade skill and trade experience, which are closely kept Burton secrets.

After a passing glance at a giant coal-scuttle in the mash-room, we went into the chamber of the hop coppers; where, in huge vessels of that rubicund metal, the hops are busily boiling with the wort. These boil together for a stated time; and then the boiling liquor comes down into a gigantic strainer. The hops left at top are pressed and sold for manure; the Excise interfering, and prying, and thwarting the brewers through the whole process. From this strainer the liquor (now become a sort of inert beer, possessing flavour but not body, bitterness without pungency,) is drawn by a prodigious arterial process of pipes into the next important stage in its career, the cooling-room. And I may mention that, while bending over the hop coppers, and watching the bare-armed perspiring men stirring them with great flat spoons or ladles, or gauging them with the mash rule, Sir John Barleycorn requested me to taste the hops, which I did, and found them to be very bitter indeed; upon which Sir John chuckled, and asked if I thought it worth while to employ strychnine, as had been grievously libelled by a certain Fench ignoramus.

I may compare the cooling-room to Behring's Straits turned brown—a sea of pale beer. On all sides—as far as the eye could reach, at least—lay this waveless, tideless sea of pale ale, traversed by an endless wooden bridge. Leaning over the balustrade of this bridge, gazing at the monstrous superficies of ale lying here a-cooling in a liquid valley, I saw myself in liquor. A good brewer, Sir John was kind enough to inform me, likes also to see himself in liquor: if his person be well-reflected in the cooling ale it is a sign that the mash has been successful. So I gazed on the ocean, and at the arterial process of pipes, at the pillars supporting the low roof, and at the flood-gates of beer far away, until, to tell the truth, the odour of the liquor made me somewhat muddy and confused, and I was not sorry when my host and guide moved forward to another department.

The wort, come to the complexion I have described, is now removed into the fermenting squares, loose boxes of beer, of plain white deal, numbered and in tiers. Here yeast is mixed with it, and the process of fermentation goes on —to what exact extent must depend, of course, on the judgment, ability, and experience of the brewer. Upon the surface of the lighter fermenting rises a thick froth, so pregnant with carbonic acid gas, that it will put a candle out, and nearly knock you down in a fainting fit if you put your nose close to it; but, being heavier than the atmospheric air, soon sinks to the bottom.

From the fermenting squares the liquor, now really pale ale, is conveyed by an intricate machinery of pipes into the cleansing or turning room. Here the casks, by hundreds and thousands, after being whirled and churned round, in order thoroughly to clean them, receive the beer, and are finally bunged and branded. They are almost immediately carted away to the railway and to London. The bottled pale ale, albeit brewed by the same process as the draught, is bottled from the wood in London, without any connexion with or reference to

Burton. The bottles have nothing to do with the brewers.

Thus ends my experience of how beer in general, and pale ale in particular, is brewed for Sir John Barleycorn at Burton-on-Trent.

LEGS.

It has always struck me that a great void exists in popular physiology from the comparative neglect with which it has treated the legs of mankind. Many and heavy folios have been written on the subject of the heart, the brain, the nerves, and the lungs. Some men have thrown themselves on the kidneys with admirable spirit and perseverance; a very large section of medical and physiological writers have devoted themselves to the stomach with an ardour and erudition worthy of our sincerest admiration; while others have attacked blood with a keen gusto and relish that have been productive of the most gratifying results to the cause of science. Sir Charles Bell wrote

an elaborate and delightful treatise on The Hand.
Still we are lamentably deficient in our knowledge of The Leg. Satisfied with the possession
of that indispensable member, our pathologists
and physiologists seem to consider it as quite
unworthy of attention; and, but for a few
meagre treatises on the gout and on varicose
veins, an occasional advertisement "To those
with tender feet," emanating from some com-
mercially-minded shoemaker, and the periodical recapitulation of the royal and noble cures
of a great corn-cutter and his brother chiropo-
dists, we might as well, for the mental attention
we bestow upon our legs and feet, be so many
Miss Biffins.

Fashion, even, that ubiquitous and capricious
visitant of the human form divine, has looked
coldly upon legs. While the shirt of man
within the last few years has undergone as
many improvements, annotations, emendations,
illustrations, and transformations as the text of
an Act of Parliament; while the human shirt-

collar has enjoyed a perfect Ovidian series of metamorphoses; whilst each succeeding season has brought changes vast and radical into the constitution of ladies' sleeves and men's wristbands; while the collars of coats and the flounces of dresses have continually changed their shapes like the chimera, and their colours like the chameleon; while the bonnet of beauty has fallen from its cocked-up elevation on the frontal bone to its accumbent position on the dorsal vertebræ; while even that conservative institution, the hat of man, has fluctuated between the chimney-pot and the D'Orsay, the wide-awake and the Jim-Crow, the Guerilla and the Kossuth, and the Garibaldi and the Spanish turban ; while all these multifarious transitions of the other parts of our garb have taken place, the coverings of the leg and the foot have been the least susceptible to the attacks of time, and fashion, and convenience. The British high-low has remained unchangeable for heaven knows how many years; the Wellington is the same boot that spurred Copenhagen's sides o'er the field of Waterloo; even the tasselled Hessian, though it has seen its coeval pig-tail sink into the limbo of oblivion, is yet worshipped in secret by devout votaries; abbreviated continuations of black silk, kerseymere, plush, corduroy, cord and leather, yet shine in the court, the diplomatic service, the servants' hall, the hunting-field, and the charity-school. Prejudice has tried to banish shorts, and Invention to improve upon stockings; the whole results of centuries of trousers wearing (the ancient Gauls wore them : see Bracchæ) have been in the ridiculous items of straps and stripes down the sides; and apparently despairing of the possibility of doing anything for legs in the improvement line, fashion has left legs alone. The world, following, like an obedient slave as it is, upon fashion's heels, has quite neglected and forgotten legs. Philosophy has turned the cold shoulder upon them; and the dramatist has scouted them, and the epic poet has disdained them. Legs have fallen to the province of mountebanks, tight-

rope dancers, acrobats, and ballet girls. From
neglect they have even fallen into opprobrium;
and we cannot find a baser term for a swindling
gambler than to call him a "Leg."

Yet only consider the immense importance of
legs! What should we be without them? Ask
that infinitely poor and miserable person, a bedridden man. To be deprived of the blessed
faculty of locomotion at will—not to possess that
glorious privilege of riding "Shanks's mare,"
or of taking the "Marrow-bone stage;" of bidding defiance to stage coaches, carriages, cabs
and railway trains; of feeling the firm earth beneath our tread; of footing it over the daisies, or
strolling over the velvetty sward, or climbing the
hill, or descending the valley, or paddling through
the brook: to be unable to take a walk, in fact,
is to be deprived of nine tithes of our pleasures
here below, of half our capacity for enjoyment,
of nearly all our faculty of observation. A man
may learn with his legs very nearly as much as
he can with his eyes; and he learns it more

cheerfully, more genially, more naturally. It
was a true word spoken in jest, that named the
legs the understandings. A great walker is
nearly always a contented, happy, and philosophically observant man. The free use of his
legs makes the penny postman satisfied with his
twenty-five shillings a-week, reconciles the policeman to his weary night watch, solaces the
sentinel on his guard, makes the ploughboy
whistle as he follows his team, the milkmaid
balance her pails merrily, and the pedlar carry
his pack as if it were a pleasure. Legs are a
consolation in trouble, and the grand remover of
spleen, care, and evil humours. The first thing
that a man does when he is immured in jail
is to walk about (if so he be allowed) his prison
yard. If you have been angry with your brother,
or if your wife has vexed you, or your affairs are
in gloomy case, or your periodical hatred of the
world and those that are in it come upon you,
you cannot do better than " walk it off."

In infancy what intense interest is concen-

trated upon legs! We watch the first endeavours
to walk of a little child with as much, if not
more, interest and anxiety than its first attempts
to speak. We seem to look upon articulation as
upon one of Nature's spontaneous good gifts
which will come in its own good time; but to
teach the child the use of its legs, and to watch
over the proper development of his paces—from
the shaky ill-balanced toddle to the straight strong
step—seem to require all our energies and caution
and attention. Heavens! what tortures mothers
must endure, what heroic sacrifices they would
submit to, to avert the horrible possibility of
baby being bandy! However remiss science
and erudition may have been, the poorer classes
appreciate legs. They know of what infinite
service those extremities will be to the child—
how absolutely indispensable they will one day
become, in conjunction with the hands as bread-
winners. They fondle and admire their children's
legs; they recommend them passionately as objects for care and prudence to the child-nurses

who carry the babies. It is only among this strongly feeling class, and not among the apathetic rich, that I have heard such a term applied to a child's extremities as "his blessed legs."

Consider of what huge importance legs are to high as well as low. Lord Viscount Protocol, sitting down on the Treasury Bench, is but a mean little man with a broad-rimmed hat pulled over his eyes; but, "on his legs," he is Cicero in eloquence, Demosthenes in delivery, Grattan in force of invective. The due management of the legs is the soul of military discipline: an army that did not keep step would be beaten by a Calmuck corporal. Legs carry the hod up ladders, with the mortar that cements the stones of our Victoria Tower. The agile use of our legs will remove us from within the deadly presence of the officer of the Sheriff of Middlesex, munished with a warrant for our arrest, and will convey us swiftly out of his bailiwick—a process of evasion denominated "leg bail."

The leg is the most honoured part of the body. It opens the ball with queens; its foot treads the carpet of thrones; without it Edward the Third could never have instituted the most honourable Order of the Garter. Do you think the Pope's Legate is so called because he is *legatus* sent? No! it is because of his legs clothed in his cardinal's red stockings. What would Louis the Fourteenth have been without the padding on his legs and the high heels to his shoes? He would have been *le petit* Monarque. What would monumental brasses and Templars' tombs be without the crossed legs of the knights and barons? Could our coats, our vests, our continuations, have been fashioned in all ages without the cross-legged tailors? The gravity of the Turk, the wisdom of his beard, the splendour of his yataghan, the perfume of his chibouk and the aroma of his coffee, would be as naught without his papouche-feeted legs folded under him on the cushioned divan.

Passing from honour to dishonour, we must

not forget that to punish a man's legs and feet is the most dreadful infliction short of death in the East; and to know the true value of legs you should be some miserable bastinadoed Turkish or Egyptian wretch crawling on your stomach from the court of justice, where the Cadi has just ordered you five hundred blows of the bastinado on your feet. The human legs have it in their power to confer the most grievous insult to human honour that is known. The hand can slap, the arm can strike, the head can butt, but it is the leg that directs the foot to confer the deadly kick; and it is a retributory leg and foot that steps out the twelve paces when the kick is washed out in blood. The legs have it in their power to conduct us to the topmost rounds of Ambition's ladder; to carry us, at the head of the forlorn hope, into the crumbling smoking breach; with our legs we trample on the carcasses of our enemies; and scamper over obstacles, and run that race of fortune which, for all our legs, is not always to the swift; with our huge legs we "bestride the narrow world like a Colossus," and make petty men creep under them.

But, O! our legs often play us sorry tricks. Bad legs, wicked legs, untrustworthy legs, they lead us to sorrow and shame, and danger and death. Ensign Whitefellow would have been as brave a young officer as ever waved a pair of colours, but for those pusillanimous legs of his, which ran away with him so shamefully at the siege of Ticonderago. It was Private Swabbins's knavish legs that caused him to abscond from barracks with his regimental necessaries; it was those same legs that took him to a marine-store shop in Back Lane, Chatham, where he sold said necessaries; and what but his legs enticed him to the beer-shop, where he spent his ill-gotten earnings? It was his legs that brought him to be tried by court-martial, and that conducted him to the military prison at Fort Clarence. Those that have sinned by their legs suffer by the legs; as the shameful stocks, and the galleries of the French bagnes, and the manacled convicts of our

dockyards, and the leg-chained street-sweepers
of the Italian towns can testify. Those likewise,
who abuse their legs by running about to strange
ale-houses, and standing at gin-shop bars, first
get unsteady on their legs, and then their legs
slide away from under them, and forsake them
utterly, and they fall into the shame of the gutter,
and the ignominy of the mud. Badly-disposed
legs carry otherwise virtuously minded men into
gambling houses, broils and contentions; they
lead them in quarrels to interpose, by which they
oft-times get an ensanguined nose; finally, dissipation must have legs, else how would it enable
its votaries to "run through" their property, and
"outrun the constable?"

The times have been when the legs have not
been deemed unworthy of performing sacerdotal
functions. Many were the choregraphic solemni-
ties of the old temples of Eleusis and Ephesus
and Memphis. The priests of Baal had sacerdotal
orgies. The witches in Macbeth danced. The
Fakirs of India leap, and the Dervishes of Stam-

boul whirl on the tips of their toes; and there are Hindoo fanatics who hope to go to heaven by standing, flamingo-wise, upon one leg.

How many and what magnificent fortunes have been made by nothing but legs? Clad in pink tights, those extremities have gathered millions of golden pieces from the opera stage. Say, ye Anatoles, ye Vestrises, ye Carlotta Grisis, ye Taglionis married to Russian princes, ye Cerritos, ye Elsslers and ye Duvernays, what would you have been without your legs? Say, ye English and continental managers, how often have you escaped bankruptcy through the legs of your figurantes and the judicious selection of ballets, otherwise "leg pieces." Captain Barclay walked himself into a comfortable annuity; and I understand that more than one professional pedestrian has realized a handsome competency by moving their legs a thousand miles in a thousand hours, in the presence of thousands of spectators at a shilling a head.

Setting riches on one side, what numbers of

industrious persons there are who earn their daily bread by their legs. At the very moment I write a company of acrobats are vaulting, leaping, tumbling, climbing, standing with their legs on each other's heads beneath my window. At an adjoining exhibition hall, Professor Squadaccini, and his three talented sons, nightly tie their legs into knots, and raise them to a level with their shoulders for a living. Madame Saqui has supported herself on her legs (on the tight-rope) since the days of the first French Revolution. Blondin, by virtue of the same accessories, realises as large an income as a Cabinet Minister. Clowns, rope-dancers, tumblers, and mountebanks of every description, would starve were it not for their legs. Even the ragged little street Bedouin who tumbles cartwheels by the side of your cab as you come from the railway-station; the brown-faced, ragged, scarlet-jacketed varlet who follows the hounds with bare feet; the Ethiopian Serenaders, who reverberate the tambourines on their knees, their shins, and the soles of their feet; the little Highland-dressed children who dance on the scrap of carpet in the muddy street, all look to their legs, as an auxiliary, if not a means, of subsistence. Nay, the piteous cripple of Italian extraction, who sits in the truck beside the barrel organ upon which the other exile grinds melancholy tunes; the stunted Jack-in-the-water paddling about, without legs, in his little canoe; and the legless beggar on the little platform on rollers who pushes himself along by means of instruments, something between dumb-bells and railway buffers, support themselves indefinitely by their legs; for passers-by remember sympathisingly that they had legs once, and relieve their leglessness with moneys.

If the heart be the stronghold of vitality, the legs are the outposts of life. The legs die first. The outposts are captured before the citadel is stormed. Mrs. Quickly put her hand upon poor dying Sir John Falstaff's legs, and they were "as cold as a stone." We speak of a man likely to die, that he will come out of the house "feet

foremost." We say of one that is dead, that he
he has " turned his toes up." No one can mistake a dead man's legs. Put them in fishermen's
boots, swathe them in fifty yards of sheeting, and
you could not mistake them. Not many days
since, at my dear old Dumbledowndeary, a man
fell from the topmast of a Dutch vessel in the
river on to the deck. They brought him to the
jetty in a boat, covering the body with a tarpaulin, while medical assistance was sent for. I can
see now the cold, gloomy grey February day; the
knot of idlers on the jetty, a solitary gull rising
from the marshes opposite with dull flapping
wings and swaying fitfully in the rising tide
beneath, the wounded man lying at full length
in the boat, and, standing on the thwarts over
him, one of his messmates, a clumsy tallow-faced
Dutchman, with a huge fur cap and earrings,
who was wringing his honest tarry hands and
crying out that he loved him; all the while the
tears trickling down his face and pattering
sharply, like commencing rain, as they fell on

the tarpaulin. But we needed not the verdict of the doctor to know that the man in the boat was dead. None but a dead man could have had the legs, stark, stiff, awful, which we saw protruding from the tarpaulin as the boat rowed to shore.

I am not at all a believer in "graphiology," and have never been tempted to send specimens of my handwriting, accompanied by a certain number of postage stamps, to Professor Anybody. Neither do I hold by those theorists who assert that all bald-headed men ill-treat their wives; neither do I swear by those who believe that all red-headed people are hypocrites. But I am a believer in the idea that a man's character can be tolerably well deciphered from his face; and I would advise all physiognomists who are of my opinion, to extend their scrutiny from a person's visage to his legs. The advantages to science would be incalculable. I have found it of prodigious service to me in my speculations upon the characters of mankind. There are as infinite varieties of expression in legs as in faces, and I wait with impatience for the day when some learned man shall give to the world an elaborate commentary on all the legs he has met with: the long and the short, the thick and the thin, the bandy and the bow, the in-kneed and the out-toed.

We are told that we can tell a man by the company he keeps; why not by the legs that take him into that company?

CHAMBERS IN THE TEMPLE.

FIVE-AND-TWENTY years ago, when I was a schoolboy in Paris, wearing a uniform very much resembling that of a Metropolitan policeman (the dress is military now, and they have metamorphosed my old college into an Imperial Lyceum), eating a distressing quantity of boiled haricots, washed down by the palest of pink wine and water, and conjugating a prodigious quantity of verbs, regular and irregular—the tenses of which have become so very preterpluperfect since, that they have faded clean away from my memory—five-and-twenty years, then, since, there was an old gentleman inhabiting the English, or St. Honoré quarter of the French capital—a white-headed, stormy, battle and weather-beaten veteran of the salt sea

—a rear-admiral in the English navy, and on the
half-pay thereof. He had been celebrated all
over the world in his time for deeds of daring and
chivalrous bravery; but that had been a very
long time ago; and the ungrateful generation
among whom his latest years—those that were
to be but labour and sorrow—were passed, celebrated only his eccentricities, and ignored or were
indifferent to his glory. This is the way of the
world, my Christian friend. When you and I
come to be old men—and should we ever have
given the world cause to talk about us—we shall
find that the books we have written, the pictures
we have painted, or the statues we have hewn,
will be dismissed to oblivion with a good-natured
contempt, as things meritorious enough in their
way, but quite out of date; should we be worth
paragraphs, or anecdotes, they will have reference
to the redness of our noses, the patterns of our
trowsers, our manner of eating peas with our
knives, our habit of putting the left leg foremost
when we walk, or our assumed fondness for cold

rum and water. The Duke of Marlborough's
petty avarice and hagglings with the Bath-chair-
men were talked about long after the conqueror
of Blenheim was forgotten, and the nation had
even grumbled about paying for the palace it had
voted him in the first outburst of its gratitude.
Lord Peterborough walking from market in his
blue ribbon, with a fowl under one arm, and a
cabbage under the other, quite threw into the
shade Lord Peterborough the hero of Almanza.
Whenever the name of the Marquis of Granby
occurs to us now-a-days, it is in connection with
the Incorporated Association of Licensed Vic-
tuallers, with foreign wines, beer, and tobacco—
not with battles won, or sieges successfully conducted. Whose aquiline nose, white ducks, and
hat-saluting fingers, were household words in
London to the populace, who had forgotten
Waterloo, when they smashed the windows of
Apsley House with stones, because its owner was
an enemy to Reform? Whose children grin now
at the caricatured presentments of the prominent

nose and plaid trousers of the man who was the greatest orator, the greatest advocate, the greatest reformer of the law, England has ever seen, and who thirty years since shook this realm from end to end by the thunder of his eloquence, and dashed down walls of corruption, one after another, with his impetuous hand? The world is as ungrateful, as fickle, as petulant as a woman. I warrant Omphale rapped the fingers of Hercules when, sitting at her feet a-spinning, he happened to ravel the flax. He who had vanquished the Nemæan lion, and quelled the Erymanthian boar, was forgotten in the careless spinner. So it was with the old gentleman whom I knew in Paris fifteen years ago. People talked of the strange fancy he had of leading an old white horse about the streets, on which he never rode; much merriment was excited by the rumour that he slept with his head through a hole in a blanket —(I am not exaggerating)—the quid nuncs of the Rue St. Honoré and the Champs Elysées were infinitely amused at his strange ways, his loud and rambling talk, his general oddity of manner; very few people cared to remember that before most of them were born he was famous over the whole world as the English Commodore Sir Sidney Smith, the heroic defender of Acre, the scourge of the French navy—from the lofty three-decker to the smallest chasse-marée,—and nearly the only man for whom the great Napoleon —the impassible, ambitious, who no more deigned to love or hate men, with him, or against him, any more than Mr. Staunton, the chess-player, loves or hates the pawns in his game—condescended to entertain a violent personal dislike. Sir Sidney Smith used coolly to declare that Napoleon was jealous of him. It is certain that he annoyed and chafed the Great Man horribly, and in Egypt drove him to the perpetration of a very sorry joke, having positively challenged him to single combat, which Napoleon declined, till— having rather an exalted idea of the "foeman worthy of his steel"—he could produce the ghost of the great Duke of Marlborough.

Sir Sidney Smith died in Paris; but it is not with his death or latter days that I have to do. I wish to tell the story of his escape from certain chambers which he occupied in the Temple, while he was yet the famous Commodore, admired by Europe, and hated by the French Directory, and especially by General Bonaparte. How much of strict historic truth there may be in the story, it is not for me to say. The journals of the period tell pretty nearly the same tale; but even newspapers will occasionally err, and even the buckets of grave history writers often stop short of the bottom of the well of verity.

Sir Sidney Smith, taken prisoner in a daring cutting-out expedition on the coast of Brittany, was confined in the prison of the Temple in Paris, in the year seventeen hundred and ninety-eight. Some idea may be formed of the importance which the republican government attached to his capture and detention, from the fact, first, that the Directory refused to liberate him in exchange for M. Bergeret, a post-captain in the French navy,

and again, on another occasion, positively refused
to receive as an equivalent for his person no fewer
than twelve thousand French prisoners! A man
worth ten thousand pounds is something; but a
sea captain not to be bought for twelve thousand
fighting men is, indeed, rich and rare.

Unfortunately, even distinction has its embar-
rassments, and such was the store set by the safe
keeping of Sir Sidney by his captors, that his
confinement was of the most rigorous description.
Verdun or Biche was good enough for ordinary
prisoners of war; but the redoubtable Commodore
was transferred to the Tower of the Temple—that
gloomy revolutionary Bastile, the scene of the
last days of Louis the Sixteenth and Marie
Antoinette, and of the slow agony and death of
the poor little captive Dauphin—the tower that
was afterwards to witness the darkest episodes of
the Consulate—the reported suicides, but whispered murders of Pichegru and Captain Wright
—the last adieux of the simple, yet desperate,
Chouans — the stern presence of their leader

Georges Cadoudal. In the Temple, then, Sir Sidney Smith was incarcerated. The guards were doubled, the defences strengthened, all communication from without was denied him, and the most rigid surveillance was exercised over all his actions.

Once having got their prisoner safe within the four strong walls of the Temple, however, isolated him from all exterior influences, and placed a strong guard over him, the Directory did not feel it necessary to treat him with any great personal severity. They did not load him with chains, they did not lock him up in a dungeon, they did not feed him upon bread and water. Sir Sidney was amply provided with pecuniary resources, and was allowed to keep himself. Apartments, the most commodious that the prison could afford, were allotted to him, and, furthermore, he was allowed to maintain something like an establishment of domestics. Besides Captain Wright, who acted as his secretary, he had a cook, a valet, and notably an English servant, half groom, half confidential man, called Sparkes. The cook and valet were freemen, and Frenchmen; Sparkes had been taken prisoner at the same time as the Commodore, but the condition attached to the French who were permitted to attend upon Sir Sidney was, that they should share his imprisonment—not one was permitted to pass the outer gate of the Temple.

I am not aware whether it has ever been the lot of any of the ladies or gentlemen who read this to have suffered the slow torture of imprisonment. I hope not; but if any such there be, they will readily understand how prone is the human mind, when the body is incarcerated, to devote itself to the culinary art. Most prisoners are good cooks, or, at least, love good eating. The man with the iron mask was a gourmand. The sham Dauphin (one of the nine hundred and ninety-nine sham Dauphins) who called himself Duke de Normandie, and had passed three-fourths of his existence in the different prisons of Europe, was renowned for the confection of roast turkey stuffed with chestnuts. When confined in Ste. Pélagie, in eighteen hundred and thirty-three, it was a matter of daily occurrence to hear a cry from his fellow prisoners of "Capet, is the turkey nearly ready?" and the pseudo-descendant of St. Louis would answer, "I am dishing it." The late Mr. Rush, on the memorable occasion of his trial, addressed a very specific and emphatic billet-doux from his retreat in Norwich Castle to the eating-house keeper opposite, commanding pig, "and plenty of plum sauce." I have seen in Whitecross Street prison an analytical chemist frying pancakes, and it was once my fortune to know, in the Queen's Bench, a doctor of divinity whose mock-turtle soup would have rather asto-nished Mr. Farrance of Spring Gardens. Now, though Sir Sidney Smith on shipboard would have been perfectly content with ship's cookery, —salt junk, salt horse, or salt mahogany, as it is indifferently called; plum duff, grey pea-soup, sea-pie, lobscouse, weevilly biscuit, and new rum —no sooner did he find himself immured in the

Temple, than he fell into the ordinary idiosyncrasy of prisoners, and became an accomplished bon-vivant. The choicest of fish, flesh, and fowl were procured from the Parisian market, and (after being strictly examined at the gate to see whether they contained any treasonable missives) furnished forth, by no means coldly, his prison table. The famous roast beef of Old England was seen, and smoked within those gloomy walls. Sir Sidney had endless disputes with the French cook concerning the thickness of melted butter, the propriety of potatoes appearing at table with their skins on; the injury done to a rumpsteak by beating it; the discretion necessary in the employment of garlic, and the number of hours necessary to be devoted to the boiling of a plum-pudding. The cook would *not* boil it long enough. Unless closely watched, he would withdraw it furtively from the pot, hide it in secret places till dinner-time, and declare stoutly that it had been boiling eight hours when it had not been three on the fire. But, errors excepted, the captives lived

as well as those bellicose bipeds of the gallinaceous breed, whose spur-combats were formerly
the delight of our British nobility, are popularly
supposed to live. Nor were good liquids wanting
to wash down these succulent repasts. For the
first time, perhaps, in France that noble com-
pound, the punch of the United Kingdom (for
England, Scotland, and Ireland are all equally
famous for it) was brewed within the prison walls;
and every Frenchman who tasted it—even the
rabidest enemy of " Pitt et Cobourg "—thenceforth renounced the small-beer julep, half sour,
half syruppy, thitherto misnamed " punch "
abroad. Brandy, sherry, and claret also formed
part of the Commodore's cellar, and, in particular,
he had laid in a supply of admirable old port
wine—rare old stuff—bottles of liquid rubies, in
a setting of rich crust and cobwebs. Money can
do almost anything in any times. It can break
the sternest of blockades, and, though it could
not get Sir Sidney Smith out of prison, it could
procure him a supply of the primest wines in

the English market. The French cook admired the old port wine hugely. He discovered that "porto" was required for a great many dishes and sauces. He was discovered in the kitchen one day by Sparkes, weeping bitterly into a stew-pan, by the side of an empty port wine bottle, He declared on that occasion, with some thickness of utterance, that the Directory were brigands, and the National Assembly thieves, and that the name of the legitimate ruler of France was Louis the Eighteenth. He was very pale and shaky next day, affected great republican sternness, and insisted more than ever upon being called "citizen," and "Junius Brutus," when, honest man, his name was Jean Baptiste all over, from his slippers to his white nightcap. These details may probably seem useless; but the Commodore's port wine had more to do with his escape from his chambers in the Temple than you may at present imagine.

One gilt and burnished afternoon in the autumn of this same year 'ninety-eight, a party of four persons were assembled in Sir Sidney Smith's sitting-room in the Tower of the Temple. One of these persons was Captain Wright, whom, as he has nothing further to do with this history, I need not specially describe. The second was Sir Sidney Smith, then in all the pride and vigour of his manhood—a little pale, perhaps, through want of exercise, but a comely man, and fair to look upon. He had his hair powdered, and wore top-boots, which would seem somewhat strange articles of costume for a naval officer, albeit in plain clothes, in these days, but were the fashion in 'ninety-eight. The third was Mr. Sparkes, his body servant. Mr. Sparkes was of the middle height, and remarkably stout, though anything but corpulent in the face. He was so stout about the chest, that you could scarcely divest yourself of the impression that he had more than one waistcoat on. Perhaps he had. A very low forehead had Mr. Sparkes, and a very voluminous allowance of bushy red hair. He was freckled, and his chin was lost in the folds of his

ample cravat. He had a considerable impedi-
ment in his speech, which caused him to speak
slowly, and not often, and not much at a time;
but he was a great humorist, and was an enormous favourite among the prison officials for his
droll sayings, and for the hideously execrable
manner in which he pronounced the French
language. A thorough Briton—an incorrigible
"rosbif" was Sparkes, said they—there were
some hopes of the Commodore acquiring a decent
knowledge of French after a few years' residence,
but as for Sparkes, he would never learn, not he.
Doctor Jollivet, the prison surgeon, who had been
in England, and spoke ravishing English, declared John as "tout ce qu'il y avait de plus
Coqueni "—by which, it is to be presumed, he
meant Cockney. Sparkes had been brought up,
he said, with the Commodore, which accounted for
a certain degree of familiarity with which he
treated him, and which he was far from showing
to the other servants. This present golden
afternoon John half stood behind his master's

chair, half leaned against the side-board. He was attentive in supplying the wants of the other persons present, but he did not neglect to help himself liberally from a special bottle of port behind him, nor did he refrain from joining, from time to time, in the conversation.

The fourth person of this group, and who sat at the end of the table facing the Commodore, was a Frenchman,—a very important person, too, you are to know, being Citizen Mutius Scævola Lasne (formerly Martin), concierge, keeper or head gaoler of the Temple. He was responsible for the safe keeping of the prisoners with his head. He slept every night with the prison keys under his pillow. He knew where the secret dungeons—the underground cachots and caba-nons—were, and what manner of men were in them. He was not a man to be despised.

Citizen Lasne was a very large, fat man, with a small head. Gaolers generally are,—but let that pass. Now there is no medium of character or disposition in large fat men with small heads. They are either intolerably vicious, slowly cruel, stolidly hard-hearted, mischievously stupid, torpidly revengeful, dully selfish, sensual and avaricious, or else they are lazy, good-natured, genial, soft-hearted giants, — mere toasts and butter, giving freely, lending freely, spending freely, always ready to weep at a pitiful tale, to sing the best song they know, to lend you their best umbrella, and to walk wheresoever you wish to lead them. It is the same with bald-headed men who wear spectacles. They are either atrocious villains or amiable philanthropists. The races admit of no mediocrity. Citizen Lasne happened, luckily for his prisoners, to be a large fat man, of the second or soft-hearted category. His exterior was rugged and his moustache was fierce. He was as stupid as the libretto of an opera, and as vain as a dab-chick; but his nature was honest, simple, confiding, and compassionate. He was the foolish, fat scullion of Sterne metamorphosed into a man. He would have spared a

flea when he caught him,—a three-bottle flea,
drunk with his life blood, and giddy with leaping
over his body. He would do anything for a prisoner save allow him to escape,—for, like all slow
men, he had a fixed idea, and this fixed idea confirmed him in, and kept continually before him,
the conviction that one prisoner the less in the
Temple (unless legally discharged), was one head
the less upon his own shoulders. This is why he
always inspected the bolts, bars, and locks of the
doors and windows every night, set the watch,
and slept with the keys of the Temple under his
pillow.

Citizen Lasne liked drink. For port wine he
conceived an immoderate affection. His liking
for that beverage was pleasingly gratified, as the
Commodore frequently invited him to his table.
Misery makes us acquainted with strange bed-
fellows, and a gaol makes a man take up with
strange boon companions. These eyes have seen
the son of an Earl hob-nobbing at a prison tap
with an insolvent boot-closer. On his own

quarter-deck, in London, at St. James's, Sir
Sidney Smith would doubtless have been as dig-
nified, not to say haughty, as an Englishman and
a Commodore has a right to be. In the state
cabin of his own flag-ship he would decidedly not
have hob-nobbed with Bob Catskin, the boat-
swain's mate. But a prisoner in the Temple, far
from home, almost solitary, any companionship
was welcome to him. This is why he so often
invited Citizen Lasne to dinner and to supper.
This is why that fat citizen sat facing him at the
table on the golden autumn afternoon I treat of.

The citizen having eaten like an ox (he approved of English cookery much), was now
drinking like a fish. He could stand a prodigious quantity of drink,—all fat men can. Only
as he drank, his eyes, which were small and
round, appeared to diminish still further in
volume, for the little penthouses of his eyelids
began to droop somewhat, and his round rosy
cheeks to puff out upwards and laterally, while
the eyes themselves seemed to recede into their

orbits, as though they were lazy with repletion, and were throwing themselves back in their easy-chairs.

The table was covered with plates of fruit and decanters of wine, from both of which Citizen Lasne was helping himself largely,—the others in moderation. The citizen drank his old port out of a tumbler,—the starveling and effeminate thimblefulls known as English wine-glasses not having as yet penetrated into the Temple. He-persisted in calling the port "a little wine,"—un petit vin délicieux,—meanwhile taking hearty gulps of the libelled liquor; for it is a mighty and generous wine,—yea, that invigorateth the frame, and maketh the hearts of men strong within them. It hath cheered the vigils of great scholars, and armed brave warriors for the fray, —port wine. As the citizen drank, however, it was evident that the fixed idea was anything but dormant within him; for he watched his host's countenance from time to time narrowly, and in the midst of his hilarity and talkativeness their

would occasionally flit across his fat face an expression almost of alarm,—for Sir Sidney was
taciturn, pensive, evidently pre-occupied, drank
little, and leant his head on his hand.

"May I pass for a 'suspect,'" he cried suddenly, laying-down his glass, "if I drink another
drop."

"What's the matter, Father Latchkey?" asked
Mr. Sparkes in French, far too ungrammatical to
transcribe here. "Wine gone the wrong way,—
swallowed a fly? Why, you look as if you saw a
file in the bottom of your glass, and a bunch of
skeleton keys in the Commodore's face."

"May I sneeze in the sawdust" (when a
person is guillotined, his head falls into a basket-
full of sawdust) "if the citizen prisoner of war
is not thinking of his Three Muses at this very
moment."

The "Three Muses" were three royalist ladies,
hiding their real names under the fabulous sobri-
quets of Thalia, Melpomene, and Clio, who had
long and successfully evaded the pursuit of the

police, and who were notoriously continually conspiring to effect the deliverance of Sir Sidney Smith. It should be known that at this period, notwithstanding the sanguinary severity of the Republican government against the Royalists, France and Paris swarmed with secret emissaries from foreign powers, known as " alarmists," " accapareurs ; " but more under the generic name of " agents de l'étranger," and by the populace as " Pitt-et-Cobourgs." There were agents from London, from Vienna, from Berlin, and from Amsterdam. There were agents in the army, the navy, the salons, the public offices, the antechambers of the ministry; among the box-openers at theatres, the market-women in the Halle, the coachmen on the stand,—all well supplied with money, all indefatigable in obtaining information, in fomenting reactionary disturbances, in promoting the escape of political prisoners. I might fill a book with anecdotes of Conrad Kock, the Dutch banker (guillotined); Berthold Proly (guillotined); the two Moravian brothers Frey,

and their sister Léopoldine; André-Marie Guz-
man, the Spaniard, who actually so far ingratiated
himself into the confidence of Marat that the last
letter the famous terrorist ever wrote was to him;
Webber, the Englishman, whose mission it was to
obtain plans of French fortified towns, and paid
twelve thousand francs for one of Douai; one
Greenwood, who was specially employed to give
dinners to distressed Royalists; Mrs. Knox; and
especially the two famous Pitt-et-Cobourgs, Dick-
son and Winter, who braved the Terror, the
Directory, the Consulate and the Empire, and
only gave up business in eighteen hundred and
fifteen. It was pretty well known to the police,
when our fat friend alluded to the Three Muses,
that an intricate and elaborate network of in-
trigues, plots and counterplots, existed for the
release of Sir Sidney Smith; that neither money
nor men were wanting to effect this, should an
opportunity occur; and that persons secretly
powerful were working night and day to bring
that opportunity about. This is why the English

Commodore had been so particularly recommended to Citizen Lasne, and why the fixed idea I have mentioned was so prominent in that patriot's mind.

"You will pardon me, Citizen Commodore," the gaoler continued, rising, but casting a loving look at the decanters, "but I don't like to see you look thoughtful. Thinking means running. I must go and examine all the locks, and order the night-watch to be doubled."

"A man may be thinking of his home and friends, his King and country, without meditating an escape there and then, my good Lasne," Sir Sidney said with a quiet smile.

"Ah," objected the gaoler, shaking his fat head, "but you've too many friends in Paris, citizen prisoner. Your King sends too many guineas and spies over here. There are hundreds of them between here and the Rue St. Antoine at this moment, I'll be bound. Very kind indeed to think of your friends, but if you should feel inclined to say bonjour to them, my only friend would be Charlot (the public executioner)."

If Citizen Lasne could have spoken English, and have made a pun, he might have said that that only friend would have cut him. But he was a stupid fat man, and could do neither.

"Make your mind easy, my friend," replied Sir Sidney Smith, "I will promise you not to escape to-night."

"You promise! then it's all right: you promise, mind," ejaculated Citizen Lasne, joyfully.

"I give you my word."

"Then give me some more wine," cried this merry fat man. "More Porto, Monsieur Spark, my dear, ho! ho!"

With which he sat down, and held out his tumbler with his great fat doughy hand, that looked as if it had just been kneaded, and was ready for the bakehouse.

"More port, more port," grumbled, or pretended to grumble Mr. Sparkes, filling the bacchanalian's glass to the brim; "what an old forty-stomach it is. He blows his windbags out like a sail. There'll be bellows to mend before long. Here's more port for you."

" 'Tis good, my friend, 'tis an exquisite little wine. Yet a little more. A drop—guggl-gl-gl-gl " —and he continued to drink.

The gaolor knew that Sir Sidney Smith was a man of inflexible honour and integrity; that to him his word as a sailor, a knight, a gentleman, was sacred. So he put the fixed idea out to grass for a time, and drank more port.

But port, though an exquisite little wine, will tell its tale, and have its own way with a man at last, like labour, like age, like death. The Citizen Lasne became very talkative indeed, which showed that he was getting on; then he sang a song, which showed that he was getting further on; then he essayed to dance, which showed that he was getting drunk; then he told a story about a pig in the South of France, and cried: which showed that he was very drunk indeed.

"Citizen Commodore," he said all at once,

"would you like to take a walk on the Boulevard?"

At this strange proposition Sir Sidney turned his eyes to the barred window. The rays of the setting sun threw the shadows of the bars upon the wall: the bright light was between. And the gentle breeze of the evening came into the room like the whisper of an angel.

The hum and murmur of the great city came up and smote the captive upon the ear, gently, lovingly, gaily, as though they said, "Come, why tarry? you are invited." And the birds were singing outside upon the gloomy terrace, where the little Dauphin used to walk.

"Monsieur Lasne," answered the Commodore, stifling a sigh, "there are subjects upon which it is both unjust and cruel to jest."

"But I'm not jesting."

"But do you really mean to say that you would consent . . ."

"Once more, would you like to take a walk on the Boulevard?"

" Would you like to take a walk on the Boulevard?" bawled Sparkes, applying his mouth to
his master's ear, as though he were deaf.

" If you are speaking seriously," Sir Sidney
said at last, "I can but accept the offer with the
greatest gratitude."

" Seriously, of course I am," replied Citizen
Lasne, rising, and shaking off the load of port
wine from his fat form, as though it were a cloak,
and really succeeding in standing straight.
" First, though, let us make our little conditions.
No attempts at escape."

" Oh, of course not," replied the Commodore.

" No speaking to any one you meet on the
road. No Muses; no words, gestures ; not a nod,
not a wink."

" I promise all this."

" On the word of an honest man."

" On the word of an English gentleman," answered the Commodore firmly.

" Come along then," cried the gaoler, as if
perfectly satisfied, linking his arm in that of his

prisoner, and moving towards the door: "you shall see of what stuff the Boulevards of Paris are made, Citizen Commodore."

Although this fat turnkey had drunk a prodigious quantity of port wine, he did not seem, once on his legs, so very much the worse for liquor. He gave one of his legs a little pat as if to reproach it for having been shaky, and took a last gulp of port by way of a final clench or steadier. Only his little eyes began to flame and sparkle greatly, which from the general dulness of his countenance gave him the appearance of having an evening party inside his head, and having had the windows lighted up.

The pair were going out when Citizen Lasne was aware of Mr. Sparkes, who leaned against the sideboard with his arms folded, looking anything but contented with the general aspect of affairs.

"A citizen who has poured me out so many tumblers of good wine," said the gaoler, graciously, "deserves some little consideration at my hands. Pass your word for him too, Commodore, and Citizen Spark shall come with us."

"You have my word," Sir Sidney said, laughing. "Sparkes shall make no attempt at escape."

"You might have asked me for *my* word," grumbled Mr. Sparkes. "That would have been quite sufficient. A nice Republican you must be to think that the word of a gentleman's servant is not as good as that of a gentleman. Is that your fraternity, or equality, or whatever you call it?"

"Liberty, equality, and fraternity," replied Citizen Lasne, with vinous gravity, "are very pretty to look at on the two-sous pieces; but the heart of man is deceitful. However," he added, "may I pass for a ci-devant, Citizen Spark, if I think that you would play me false. Citizen, come along. Citizen Secretary (to Captain Wright) I recommend myself to your distinguished consideration till we return. Au Boulevard!"

He led the Commodore away, and Sparkes

followed close at their heels, as a well-bred gentleman's servant should do. A few minutes afterwards the three were outside the great gate of
the Temple. The Commodore had taken care to
wrap himself in a cloak, and to slouch his hat
over his head. As long as the sun remained
on the horizon the party wandered about the
Dædalus of narrow little streets which then
surrounded, and even now to a certain extent
surround, the Temple. As it grew dark, the
Commodore proposed that they should take the
promised walk on the Boulevard.

Now Citizen Lasne, in regard to liquor, was
somewhat of a spongy nature and temperament.
He could suck up an astonishing quantity of
moisture, but such moisture was very easily
expressed by a few minutes' exercise, and then
the citizen was dry, porous, on the alert and
ready for more. When Citizen Lasne left the
Temple with his prisoners he was considerably
more than seven-eighths drunk. He had not
been long in the fresh air before the fixed idea

began to dominate over his mind with redoubled force. He began to repent of his somewhat too chivalrous confidence in the parole of his captives. He began to repent heartily of his imprudence. He began, finally, like Falstaff, to perceive that he had been an ass; and, worse than all, that he had effected that undesirable metamorphosis himself.

As they walked he scrutinised narrowly the countenances of the passers-by, to see if any marks of recognition passed between them and his companion. And almost incessantly he glanced over his shoulder to assure himself of the whereabout of Citizen Sparkes. That trusty servant was contented with treading most faithfully upon his gaolers' heels, and with saying, when he caught his eye,

"All right, Citizen—all right."

If the fumes of the wine had been completely, instead of very nearly, evaporated from the cerebellum of Citizen Lasne, he would have remarked a little circumstance which might have led him to entertain very grave suspicions concerning the safety of his prisoners. Ever since the party had quitted the Temple, they had been followed, step by step, by a female figure closely shawled and veiled; and Sir Sidney could distinctly hear, though the gaoler, from a trifling singing and buzzing in his ears, could not, the sound of steps behind them, regularly keeping time with their own.

The night was dark, and Lasne, determined to keep his word at all hazards, proceeded towards the Boulevard. At the moment when the three were turning the angle of the Rue Charlot a hand was laid on the arm of Citizen Sparkes, and a timid voice whispered—

"Monsieur le Comte."

Sparkes turned his head round, without slackening his pace.

"I saw you start," whispered the veiled female, for she was the owner of the hand and voice. "I have informed my sisters. Rochecotte and De Phélippaux are in readiness. One word and the Commodore shall be rescued from the hands of that wretch."

" But the Commodore will not say that word," answered Citizen Sparkes, in very pure and elegant French.

" And in heaven's name, why ? "

" He has given his word, as a gentleman, not to attempt to escape to-night.'

" And you——" the veiled figure continued.

" Oh, as for me—the Commodore was security for me—but——"

The night grew darker, and darker, and the three strange companions, with the phantom in the veil, were lost in the tumultuous sea of life upon the great Boulevards.

There was no Boulevard des Italiens then ; no Rue de la Paix, no Madeleine, no asphalte pavements, no brilliant passages, no gas-lamps. But the Boulevards were still the Boulevards, unequalled and unrivalled ; the crowds of promenaders and loungers were still the same, though attired in costumes far different from those they wear now. They passed some dozen of theatres, they passed Monsieur Curtius's wax-work exhibition; they passed numberless groups of tight-rope dancers, jugglers, mountebanks, learned dogs and quack docters. All at once, just as they had arrived at the spot where the Passage Vendome has since been constructed, Citizen Lasne uttered an exclamation of horror and surprise.

"By heavens!" he cried, "Spark has disappeared!"

It was but too true, the body servant of Sir Sidney Smith was nowhere to be seen.

In his terror and agitation the unlucky gaoler quite forgot his Republican character. He was within a hair's breadth of making the sign of the cross; but remembering that religion had been done away with according to law long since, he twirled his moustache instead.

"May heaven grant," said the Commodore to himself, "that the poor fellow has really succeeded in making his escape." Then he added, aloud, "Sparkes has no doubt lost us."

" Lost us," cried the concierge, furiously, "lost us!—yes, to find himself in London. I am ruined, destroyed. Citizen, citizen, I am a poor man, the father of a family, I have a head—I know I shall lose it—let us hasten home like the very devil."

He seized the Commodore's arm tightly as he spoke, and quickened his pace; and Sir Sidney had no alternative but to walk as fast as his companion. They ascended the Boulevard, and then rapidly descended the Rue du Temple.

But the tribulations of Citizen Lasne had not yet reached their culminating point. At the top of the Rue Mesaly they found the thorough-fare obstructed by a numerous crowd. Men of equivocal appearance hovered about, and formed suspicious groups. Some carts and barrows had been overturned in the roadway, evidently with the intention of forming a barricade. Lasne cast round him a desperate look. A gaoler, he scented a conspiracy from afar off.

"And where may you be taking this honest man, citizen," asked a man, placing himself directly in Lasne's way. The man wore a coarse blue blouse, but the ill-buttoned collar showed something most suspiciously like a lace shirtfrill beneath.

"Room there!" cried Lasne, to whom despair lent courage.

"You're in a hurry, Citizen Donkey. If I relieve you of the care of that ci-devant who is hanging on your arm, don't you think you could walk faster?"

"Room there!" repeated the gaoler in a hoarse voice. "Room, in the name of the Directory, in the name of the Republic——"

"One, and indivisible?" interrupted the man in the blouse. "We know all about it. Hallo! attention there!"

The groups closed up. Citizen Lasne felt himself hustled, buffetted, half strangled. Then he was violently dragged down a bye-street and thrust into a doorway. When he recovered his scattered senses, he was alone—the Commodore had disappeared.

"Oh my children, my poor children," murmured Citizen Lasne, pursuing his solitary walk towards the Temple. "What will become of them? Oh accursed be Pitt and Coburg! Oh thrice accursed be the wine of Porto!"

A fat man in a fright is not a pleasant sight to see. He always puts me in mind of a pig just poniarded by the butcher, and running about in extremis. The legs of Citizen Lasne quivered under him. A cold perspiration broke out all over him. He felt like a lump of ice in his backbone. The ends of his hair pricked his forehead; the singing in his ears loudened into a yell. The pores of his flesh opened and shut like oysters; and the whole of his inside became incontinent one mass of molten lead.

As he neared the Temple, the opposite sides of the street formed themselves into a horrible proscenium, and in the middle an infernal drama was being acted. He saw, painted all in red, somebody having the hair at the back of his head shaved off by somebody else hideously like M. Sanson, otherwise called Charlot, the public executioner; then somebody being strapped upon a plank and thrust head downwards between two posts, in grooves of which ran a huge tri-angular axe. And the axe fell with a "thud," and somebody's head fell into a red basket full of sawdust, and the fiends that were yelling in his ear called out "Citizen Lasne, Citizen Lasne, agent of Pitt-et-Coburg." And the devil danced before the theatre, playing upon a pipe.

The unhappy gaoler reached the Temple gate. He rang, and was about to enter, when he heard a voice behind him.

" Will you permit me also to enter, Monsieur Lasne ? "

The citizen could hardly believe his ears. Much harder was it for him to believe his eyes, when turning round, he recognised Sir Sidney Smith.

"May I be consumed," (he used a stronger

term than this), cried Citizen Lasne, "if the word of a gentleman is not worth all the bolts and bars in the Temple."

Notwithstanding his high eulogium upon a gentleman's word, Citizen Lasne did not forget to see the bolts and bars properly secured as soon as he got inside. But a vigorous pressure from without prevented the closing of the great door, and a voice was heard crying,—

"Let me in! let me in! 'Tis I, Sparkes."

"And where the wonder," (he used even a stronger term this time), "do you come from?" asked Citizen Lasne, when the Commodore's body-servant had been admitted.

"Where! why from looking after you to be sure. Do you call this fraternity and equality, locking a man out of his own prison? A pretty country, where, instead of prisoners running away from the gaolers, the gaolers run away from the prisoners."

Citizen Lasne was too delighted at the safe recovery of his prisoners to resent Mr. Sparkes's reproaches. He insisted upon lighting the Commodore to his apartments; he overwhelmed him with compliments and thanks. He positively wanted to embrace him. The Commodore repulsed him gently.

"You owe me nothing, M. Lasne," he said. "I had promised, I have kept my word. But dating from this moment I withdraw my parole."

"Wait till to-morrow," exclaimed Lasne, in a supplicating voice. "Only wait till to-morrow, Commodore, I'm so sleepy."

Mr. Sparkes pinched the arm of Sir Sidney Smith. "Give your word till to-morrow morning," he whispered.

"Well, so be it," pursued the Commodore. "Till to-morrow morning I will give my word to remain quiet. But after that I shall court the Muses as much as I please."

"I wish to-morrow morning were this day month," murmured Citizen Lasne, as he bid the prisoners good-night and left them to their repose.

"To-morrow morning may bring forth great things, Sir Sidney," remarked Mr. Sparkes, suddenly rising from the body-servant into the friend. "You have kept your word in neither escaping nor planning escape. I have kept the word you gave for me in not escaping. We shall see, we shall see."

The historian relates, with what accuracy I know not, that when Citizen Lasne had retired for good for the night, Mr. Sparkes took off no less than five waistcoats, and also relieved his arms and legs from much superfluous padding; that underneath his red hair he had some closely-cropped silky black locks; that the freckles on his face were removable by no stronger cosmetic than ordinary soap and water; and that in less than one quarter of an hour after the departure of the gaoler, the bluff English body-servant had unaccountably assumed the likeness of an accomplished French gentleman.

The next morning, very early, a yellow postchaise, drawn by four horses, drove up to the great door of the Temple. On the box sat two individuals, who at a glance could be recognised as gendarmes in plain clothes. Two more gendarmes, but in uniform, descended from the chaise, and assisted to alight no less a personage than Citizen Auger, adjutant-general of the army of Paris.

Shortly afterwards, the Commodore was sent for to the prison lodge, and there he was shown an order, signed by the Minister of the Interior, for the transfer of the persons of Sir Sidney Smith, and his servant, John Sparkes, Anglais, to the military prison of the Abbaye.

"And many a poor fellow have I seen transferred to the prison of the Abbaye, who has only left it to be shot in the Plaine de Grenelle," murmured Lasne. "However, tout est en règle,—all is correct. I will just enter the warrant in the books, if you will be kind enough to sign a receipt for the bodies of the prisoners, Citizen Auger."

The citizen signed his name to the prison register, "Auger, Adjutant-General," followed by a tremendous paraphe or flourish. He declined the escort of six men which Lasne was kind enough to offer him, saying that the four gendarmes were sufficient, and that, besides, he would depend on the honour of Sir Sidney Smith not to compromise him. The Commodore begged Lasne to accept the remainder of his stock of port wine, shook hands with him, took an affecting leave of poor Captain Wright, and with Sparkes entered the post-chaise. Citizen Auger followed; the two gendarmes in plain clothes mounted the box, and the carriage drove away. For aught Sir Sidney Smith knew, he was riding to his death.

The next morning the newspapers teemed with accounts of the audacious escape of Commodore Sir Sidney Smith from the prison of the Temple, by means of a forged order of transfer. Citizen Adjutant-General Auger was no other than the proscribed emigré, the Marquis de

Rochecotte, and the gendarmes were doubtless agents of the indefatigable Pitt-et-Coburg. As for Mr. John Sparkes, it was subsequently elicited that he was a certain Count de Tergorouac, a nobleman of Brittany, who had resided for a long time in England, and to whom it had luckily occurred, when taken prisoner, to assume the disguise of an Englishman.

The French police performed prodigies of strategy to arrest the fugitives, but all in vain. They reached Calais, crossed the Channel in a smuggling-vessel, and arrived safely in England.

As for Citizen Lasne, he could come to no harm; for, though the order was forged, the signature of the minister appended to it was undoubtedly genuine. It was never known by what stratagem the signature had been obtained. The fat citizen finished the Commodore's port wine gaily, and drank his health, and that of "ce digne Spark," in their now unoccupied chambers in the Temple.

FLAGS TO FURL.

FLAGS, pennons, banners, bribery, beer, cockades, rosettes, brass bands and bludgeons being
manifestly contrary and inimical to virtue, are to
be abolished by the strong arm of the law. They
are not in themselves, as things, essentially im-
moral; but they are vicious when taken in connection with the election of members to the
Commons House of Parliament. That assembly,
confessed to be composed of the collective wisdom
of the nation, has perhaps been held to include
also the collective national virtue; and with this
view, a Bill has been introduced, and is now
before the House,* relating to expenses at elections, in which war to the knife is waged against

* July, 1853.

every species of flag, banner, rosette, cockade,
colour, or procession, which might dare to flaunt
its drapery during, or immediately before or after,
an election. The game is up. The flags must be
furled.

Shade of George Crabbe, late of Aldborough,
clerk; shade of William Hogarth, late of Leicester
fields and Chiswick, painter, engraver, and moral-
ist; shades of Gatton and of that deathless dead
wall which once represented old Sarum, and
returned representatives to Parliament; shades
of Wilkes and Luttrell, Fox and Queensbury;
shades of all parliamentary elections past, present,
and to come, gather round me while I meditate
on this redoubted Bill! Election expenses—like
poor Scotland, as described by the Scotch gentleman in Macbeth—will not only not stand where
they did, but be almost ashamed to know themselves. No banners! no flags! no brass bands!
no bribery! no open public-houses! no party pro-
cessions! Why not as well have no candidates
—no voters—no elections? Ruthless legislators!

would you give us a marriage without white satin favours, orange flowers, Malines lace, and bride cake? Would you have a funeral without gloves and feathers, cake and wine, and disconsolate mutes (at one shilling an hour) who, after the funeral, become liquids? In a few years, we shall have not only marriages without favours, funerals without crape and sherry, and elections without banners, but royalty without beef-eaters, public offices without red tape, Lord Mayors without sword-bearers, Field Marshals without gold lace and cocked hats, and Judges without wigs. We want only the New Reform Bill with which we are threatened, and a man instead of saying, " I belong to the borough of Splitvote, or the county of Plumpshire," will say " I have a vote for group No. 6, or for section D," or for some other tabulated nonentity, into which this unhappy and ruined, but formerly Conservative country has been subdivided. Peradventure, if an antiquary or a speculator does by chance rummage out from some town-hall lumber room,

many years hence, a few tarnished banners, a few
faded streamers, a few battered dingy fragments
of electioneering paraphernalia, they will be
looked at as relics of a curious past, like the
dried fowls, old honeycombs, and tear-bottles
from the tombs of Thebes; or the winged lions
and ivory thrones from the palaces of Nineveh;
or the drinking cups and baker's loaves from
Pompeii.

And not alone to the old school will the aboli-
tion and prohibition of these constitutional insignia be a source of melancholy, discomfiture,
and foreboding. To them, furled banners, silenced
bands of music, pocketed cockades, and absent
streamers, will be merely suggestive of the im-
pending decadence of Britain. They will not,
however, drink one flagon the less, nor be a whit
less jovial; for, it is a curious trait in human character, that a man bears the misfortunes of his
country much better than he bears his own.
The ruin of the agricultural interest by fatal
tergiversation and heartless duplicity, &c. &c.

on the occasion of the last complete destruction and final overthrow of Britain, has not, to my knowledge, affected the excellent *symposia* throughout the country, known as farmers' ordinaries, or in any manner the appetites of the farmers attending thereat; nor, although it is well known that the repeal of the Navigation Laws has hopelessly crushed and annihilated the shipping interest, have I, in my experiences of shipping, ship-launches, and ship-launch-dinners, been brought into any disagreeable juxtaposition with sackcloth and ashes. On the contrary, I have more frequently met "'tween decks," with lively, long-necked individuals, tipped with tin foil by the name of Clicquot, Ruinart, Moët, and Sillery, hailing from the city of Rheims, or the province of Champagne in France.

What, will you be kind enough to inform me, is to become of Ozias Bridlegoose, Esquire, Attorney and Parliamentary Agent, of Horsenail Buildings, Derby Street, Peccable Square? That estimable gentleman has, for the last twenty

years, kept a Boroughs Engaged and a Boroughs
Engageable book with as much method and regu-
larity as a merchant keeps his double register
of bills receivable and bills payable. He knows
—he knew, at least—to a tittle what boroughs
were safe, what counties questionable, what manu-
facturing towns " no go," as clearly as a bankruptcy assignee can distinguish between good and
bad debts. Furl the flags, doff the cockades,
silence the drums and trumpets, and Mr. Bridlegoose's occupation is gone. Electoral corruption is as the air he breathes. If he have it
not, he dies.

And would you deliberately and in cold blood
immolate one of the most respected of the legal
profession, brother indeed to Mr. Serjeant Bridlegoose leader of the Sou-western circuit, who
will be a judge when the right time comes;
cousin to a Commissioner of Bankruptcy, and
nephew to the famous old John Bridlegoose, of
the no less famous firm of Bludget and Bridlegoose, the family, private, and confidential solici-

tors to that enormously wealthy but embarrassed peer, who, as he is said to owe thirty thousand pounds to his tailor, must be indebted at least half a million to his lawyers? Our Bridlegoose, the very Emperor of parliamentary agents; the Fouché, the Jonathan Wild of electoral police; shall he—in himself a Great National Institution —be utterly abolished? Has he not an army of satellites at his elbow, as numerous as the sands, as silent as death, as devoted as the affiliated of the Vehmgericht, or the myrmidons of Schinder-hannes; as discreet as Pamela; as insinuating as Sir Charles Grandison; as hypocritical as Blifil; as ferocious as Blueskin; as great masqueraders as Vidocq or the late Charles Matthews; as ac-complished linguists as Pergrade or Coutenson; as impudent as Ferdinand Count Fathom; as ubiquitous as Esmond's Father Holt; as menda-cious as George Psalmanazar: who lie like truth for his clients, and varnish truth over with lies for his adversaries?

These, Mr. Bridlegoose's merry men, scour all

boroughs. They stand at his bidding on all
hustings, platforms, and scaffolds; in all balconies, committee, club, and assembly rooms.
They parade all public-houses, taverns, gin-
palaces, and hotels. They have no master but
him, no behests but his, no virtues save fidelity
(on the Swiss principle of continuity in payment),
no passions (to speak of) save drunkenness. As
for Mr. Bridlegoose he is (or was, alas!) to the
full as ubiquitous and accomplished as his aco-
lytes. After a late dinner in St. James's Square,
or Belgravia, where the wine has circulated pretty
freely, where do you find Bridlegoose? In the
drawing-room? Far from it. Ten to one his
next appearance will be in the first-class carriage
of a night express train, soberly scanning the
second edition of the *Globe*; or, perchance, he
will be tearing in a cab through the dirty streets
of Bermondsey or Bethnal Green, or some out-of-
the-way suburb, boiling over with instructions
and packages for one of his merry men, there in
hiding; or he will be in his own paper-crammed

office in Horsenail Buildings, Derby Street, Peccable Square, giving mysterious orders to merry men not in hiding ; but who yet loom hazily behind the collars of cloaks and great-coats, and from whom there seldom issues a sound more distinct than that of an asthmatic cough or the suppressed chink of half-sovereigns.

Else would you find the impetuous Bridlegoose darting into dingy chambers in the Temple— nailing some parliamentary counsel to his table with nails of reading-lamps and old port wine, and golden fees. Presto, at almost the same time, you hear of him sliding mysteriously into some far-off country hotel late at night, ordering a private room and a bottle of sherry, and sending a note by the boots to the lawyer, or the parson, or the barber, or the head linen-draper, that a gentleman from Shropshire was waiting at the George, and wished to see him, if he pleased, directly.

What a man Bridlegoose is for cabs ! Of all men, who has so much reason to bless Mr. Fitzroy's new Act? He has always a cab, and is always in a cab, and yet the cab seems always waiting at doors for him, and the cabman seems for ever to be discoursing familiarly to the policeman in the vicinage concerning "the sight of papers that old cove do carry with him, to be sure." And yet he has a brougham of his own, which he uses pretty frequently, and which, stuffed inside and out with parliamentary and legal papers and blue bags, you are pretty sure to see waiting at the Carnack Club, guarded by a weary groom, who yawningly complains to the Club page of "being so much up o' nights 'cause of the governor's Parliament-house business." It is impossible for any man to be in more than one place at one and the same time. That we know; reason says it; science proves it. Lord Bacon would have told us so if he had thought us such fools as not to have known it without telling; yet it was currently reported—and the evidence went far to prove—that at the very time last winter that Bridlegoose was managing the

Ballygarret (county) election in Ireland, he was
conducting the great Snolbury contest in York-
shire; that he was canvassing the electors of the
Itchingmuchty burghs in North Britain; that
he was defending the Tippington election petition
(which was successful) before a committee of the
House of Commons; that he was appearing as a
witness (and a remarkably unwilling one) before
a committee of the House of Lords, respecting
the Great Shellout Bribery Case; that he was
attending to the registration of Conservative
electors before a revising barrister in a narrow
lane in Clerkenwell; that he was new slating the
roof of his cottage *orné* at Sydenham, in Kent;
taking the chair at the Farmers' Friend Society's
dinner at Marketpigton; rusticating with his
family at Hastings in Sussex; and accompanying
his eldest daughter to Nice for the benefit of his
health. If he had lived eighty years ago he
would have been hooted down as a Cagliostro or
a Count de Saint Germain. But in these days
natural magic has superseded necromancy; and

to gas, steam, iron, and activity must be attributed the greater portion of Mr. Bridlegoose's ubiquity.

Now, I ask what is to become of such a man as this if the standards of electioneering are to be furled? Remember! This is the man who brought in, in the year forty-three, the great nabob, Sambo Lack, Esquire, who was manifestly idiotic, who could not spell, and who got so tipsy on nomination-day that he had to be wheeled from the hustings on a truck; yet Bridlegoose brought him in triumphantly, defeating the redoubtable Ironsides—the man of the people—by a tremendous majority, solely and purely by the force of his (Bridlegoose's) electioneering genius, and not—as was in a base and paltry manner asserted by the opposite party—by the brute cash-force of Sambo Lack, Esquire. Remember, this is the man who gave to Parliament Lord Claude Wappentake, a nobleman of such strong Saxon lineage and tendencies, that in the excitement of his speech from the hustings, he roundly told the mob that they were nothing better than base-born churls, fit only—with iron collars round their necks —to herd swine; which undoubtedly true but imprudent words endangered his lordship's election, and drew upon him a shower-of dead cats, brickbats, and oyster-shells, that endangered and in some degree damaged, his lordship's head. Yet the undaunted Bridlegoose rescued him from this dilemma, and sent him in three days to Parliament, a knight of the shire, at the head of the poll. It was Bridlegoose who strangled the Potbury petition; else Scrubby Hedgehog, Esq., would have been lost to the country. For what?—for treating twenty voters with a quart of egg-hot a piece. Hear it, Nemesis! There was, to be sure, a trifling accusation in addition, that Mr. Hedgehog had kept all the public-houses in Potbury open for nine days; but that was not proved. It was this same Bridlegoose, who unseated the monster Billyroller, the flagitious profligate who gave a voter twopence to purchase a pot of beer with, at the corner of Brick Lane, Millington.

And finally, remember, Britons, it was Bridlegoose: Bridlegoose, the Bayard of Parliamentary
agents: Bridlegoose without fear and without reproach: Bridlegoose, the dauntless adherent of
Church and State—who, when the Zerubbabel
election was going clearly against Sir John Scribe
and Longhorn Pharisee, Esquire, and when the
Radical candidate, Sir Rabbitskin Syder, was two
hundred votes ahead—suddenly hit upon, devised,
wrote, printed, and published, that undying placard, declaring that Sir R. Syder, having owned
to a short visit to Bombay—must necessarily be
a Brahmin, a worshipper of Juggernaut, an adorer
of Buddha's tooth, a disciple of Mumbo-Jumbo,
an adept in Fetish rites, an advocate of canni-
balism, and an active member of the Stranglaboy
Thuggee Society; and which immortal placard
wound up with "Christian Husbands and Fathers,
will you vote for this Iconoclast?" (which means,
I rather believe, image-breaker ˙and not image-
worshipper, but it was a good word, and told
immensely), and was signed "A Protestant."

Was it not that stroke of Bridlegoose's genius which floored Sir Rabbitskin (who was as excellent a Christian gentleman as you would wish to meet); which drove him to leave Zerubbabel in disgust; and caused the Scribe and Pharisee party to circulate a report that he had left his bill at the Golden Gridiron Hotel to be liquidated by his committee?

What then, I ask again, is to become of Ozias Bridlegoose? To take away banners, bribery, and brass bands from such a man is to break the crutch of a cripple; it is to take the life-preserver from a burglar, to break the wand of Prospero, and to draw the false teeth of a beauty of sixty. What is such a man to do when the electioneering banner which has braved the battle and the breeze for a thousand years (more or less) has been furled? He cannot dig; to beg he is ashamed. Furl your flags, and you roll up Bridlegoose, the pride and ornament of the collective wisdom of his country! You pin him up, you label him as though he were an object of

curiosity in a museum—you put him away on a
dark shelf behind a glass; and twenty years
hence you will say, " This is a sample of the
thing called ' agent' who ' managed ' elections
when management was necessary to send two
honest men to represent their countrymen in the
great council of the nation." I have heard something in my time of justice to a neighbouring
country; and I stand out for justice to Bridlegoose. The Palace Court people had compensation made them; Deputy Chaffwax has been
ejected from office upon a splendid retiring fortune taken from the pockets of patentees; the
Hounslow Heath highwaymen, if they did not
get compensation, at least petitioned for it; now,
I want to know what patriotic member will go
down to the House, and in his place move for
an inquiry into the claims of Ozias Bridlegoose,
Esquire?

What is to become of the dim, mysterious,
legionary horde whom I have hastily alluded to
as the satellites of Bridlegoose? Take the cele-

brated Mr. Daggs for instance. Daggs was ori-
ginally, I believe, a horse-chaunter, and is to this
day a sporting character of considerable note.
After he got over his little difficulties in the
horse-chaunting line, which resulted in an appeal
to the Cæsar sitting in Basinghall Street, he
became a "frequenter of races," and described
himself as "on the turf;" on which I have no
doubt he very frequently really was, with very
little to cover him. Some success in the conduct
of the noble game, "red, black, blue, feather and
star," emboldened him to take a public-house of
the gladiatorial order, in the athletic town of
Nottingham; and it was here, in his Bonifacial
capacity, that his marvellous aptitude for electioneering was discovered by Mr. Bridlegoose,
then down in Nottingham on a little business.

He became shortly afterwards the Murat of
the Napoleon of the hustings. He gave up his
public-house and rushed from the turf to the poll
with an eagerness really surprising. Now, Daggs
had, I believe, about as much faith in any poli-

tical party as an artilleryman has in pea-shooters;
this, added to a natural inaptitude for public
speaking, rendered him averse to supporting by
any demonstration of eloquence the particular
candidature in whose favour he was enlisted.
The strength of his genius lay in invention, in re-
solution, in rapidity, and in subtlety. He would
turn an adverse voter's flank; bribe him, or, if
positively unbribable, hocus, kidnap, or mislead
him, without ever offending overtly the law or the
prophets. He was the sort of man who—if his
chief told him in London, that such and such a
party was short of such and such a number of
votes, in such and such a town, and that such
votes must be had within twenty hours—would
put five hundred sovereigns into his boots or his
umbrella, start off that minute by train without
further luggage; and, within the given time,
would bring his voters and their votes up to the
poll-booth, dead or alive. He had an art of en-
snaring all the bill-stickers in a town, and leaving
none to the opposite party; of tearing down that

party's placards should they manage to get any
pasted up; of having mud thrown at their hotels;
of getting the windows of their Committee Rooms
broken. He had a hundred aliases; Blenkinsop,
Mullington, Pots, Cheesewright, Barwise, Tolly-
more, Gutch, and the like. He had lodgings in
every district of London, and in every town in
the provinces, and had a name and a carpet-bag
in each. His metropolitan landladies believed
him to be "something in the City;" his provincial hostesses opined that he "travelled in
some line"—which, in truth, he did. At the
close of a successful election, his intimates—who
were few—declared that he would get silently
drunk in a cab, driving slowly from one public-
house to another, and being served in the vehicle.
If, on the contrary, the candidate for whom he
was employed were defeated, he would incontinently disappear, and be seen no more until,
weeks afterwards, he was found in some far-off
town, under an inscrutable incognito, working
with misanthropical energy for some new candi-

date. Now, see what Reform and Revolution do! Daggs is to be done for. Does any constitutional man in his five senses, believe that this country can hold its present position among nations, without Daggs?

Tom Beazly, too. Such a fellow for energy! Such promptitude, such daring. Tom was worth ten pounds a week (and got it), from any party. He had a pictorial eye, had Tom; and no man knew better than he how to arrange a showy procession. There was, besides, something of a culinary turn in his genius. He knew exactly how and in what proportion to sprinkle the banners, the insulting placards, the libellous effigies of the rival candidates, the clap-trap of the mottoes, the gaudiest of the devices. He would give the candidates private lists of the streets in which to stand up in their carriages while passing through; of the doors they were to bow to; of the windows they were to kiss their hands at. He knew how to bring a drunken freeholder upright to the poll, and how to prop up a drunken

flag-holder with a sober one. He was the best
fugleman in England for the hustings on nomi-
nation day. The cheers and the hooting, the
dead cats and the stale eggs, the loud crash of
music while the rival candidate made his speech,
the groans and the Kentish fire, the fight, and
the screaming, were never better done than when
Tom gave the signal. He was not, perhaps, a
" good and safe man " like Daggs; but, as com-
mandant of irregular horse, as a chief of Free
Lances, as an able unscrupulous persevering par-
tisan, he was positively unrivalled. If the flags
are furled, what is to become of Tom Beazly? and
what is to become of the country without him?

What is to become of the myriad swarms of
the miscellaneous army of understrappers? What
is to become of the " witness Buggles," who is
ostensibly a small bootmaker somewhere in North-
amptonshire; but who, it appears, has had an
occult influence over elections for five-and-twenty
years? What is to become of all the men in
drab and brown and grey; of all the men in

cloaks and macintoshes, who come like shadows at election times and so depart? What is to become of the innumerable small-fry of flag-bearers, touters, and musicians? What is to become of the noble army of election crimps and election publicans, and of that intensely reputable mob of voters (made corrupt by nobody) who sell their votes as they sell their chandlery and slops? What *is* to become of all these people thrown quite out of employment?

Furl the election flags, and furl the national standard! It is all one, believe me. England was great under Bridlegoose, England was great under Daggs, England was great under Beazly, England was great under the rest of the noble army whose occupation is to be destroyed. She really will be ruined now, though you may doubt it.

THE PARISIAN NIGHTS' ENTERTAINMENTS.

—◆—

WHEN your uncle Plappington (from whom you expect a good round sum in the fulness of time :—Heaven send the good man length of days !)—when Plappington of Cogglesbury-Regis comes to town for his yearly fortnight, and when he has completed his purchases of hops in the Borough Market, has concluded his order-taking in the dry-goods line, or commenced his fifteenth lawsuit;—when, in fact, he begins to feel comfortable, has had enough of business, and is not averse to a little pleasure—and when, after a neat dinner at the Cathedral Coffee-house, or the Tavistock, he says to you: "Well, boy James, and where are you going to take your uncle to-night, sir?" what are you to say in reply, and where are you to take your uncle Plappington? He wants amusement: not noise, not dissipation, not doctrine, nor art-delectation even, but simple diversion, recreation, cheerful unbending. You have all the world of London before you where to choose; yet I am very much mistaken if in that choice you feel not as puzzled as the useful and maligned quadruped, which ordinarily draws (attached to a costermonger's barrow) our greenstuff from market, is said to be between two bundles of hay. You propose the theatre, but your uncle has a horror of dramatic entertainments, and hopes (severely) that you never frequent such Pagan haunts. The idea of a Terpsichorean hall is simply absurd: bears may dance —your uncle never. Besides, you know what sort of Terpsichoreans indulge in the poetry of motion at that brilliantly chandeliered saloon; and it would be worth three times your legacy to apprise the immaculate Plappington that you knew even of the existence of a place where the unholy Redowa is performed, and the depraved sherry cobbler consumed. There is the Polychromatic Institution, but then, again, your uncle was born (like the Earl of Derby and Guy Fawkes) before physical science formed a part of popular invention—before gas was invented, or Vauxhall Bridge built. It would be no great amusement to him to be galvanised, to be half asphyxiated in a diving-bell, to see a luminous fountain, to be crowded in a dark amphitheatre while a learned gentleman below lectured, in broad Scotch, upon the adulterations of bole-armenian, or extracted sparks from potatoes, or sunbeams from cucumbers. He would yawn over the photographic phenomena of fern leaves, and go to sleep outright when the drop of Thames' water was magnified five million times, and the interesting monsters that inhabit the pellucid element were shown, leaping and fighting, and devouring each other, in all the hideous horror of microscopic truth. There are the two great suburban pleasure gardens; but then, one of

them never opens save when the clerk of the
weather is out of temper, and the clouds pour
down torrents of rain; and the other (your uncle
is nervous about steamboats) cannot be reached
under a two-and-sixpenny cab-fare, leaving the
return out of the question. You might take the
worthy Plappington to the Bucephalus Club, and
show him the wonders of that palatial establishment—the Sienna marble columns, the reading
and smoking rooms, the deliciously somnolent
library and the alabaster lavatories, the colossal
footmen and symmetrical foot-page—you might
win his money at whist, and hear him argue with
Colonel Flatherstone upon the prospects of the
next hop harvest—only you don't happen to be
a member of the Bucephalus; and to your own
club—the Social Sybarites—held in the long
room over the Scythian's Arms, Stagyrite Lane,
you do not like to take him, lest he should think
you addicted to beer and tobacco fumes, and lest
he should be shocked at Bob Spoffle's comic
songs, or exacerbated by Jack Bitefile's brilliant

but somewhat indiscriminate repartee. You cannot take him—no, boy James, you shall not take
him to the Cave of Harmony, or the Dusthole, or
the cellar under the Anacreon's Head. It would
but ill beseem a man of his age and standing to
be seen at a grog-stained table till three in the
morning, listening to songs inexpressibly stupid.
Where, then, is your uncle to go? To the Opera,
and pay eight-and-sixpence to hear music beyond
his comprehension, sung to words in a language
he doesn't understand? To the coffee-room of
an hotel, to drone over the evening papers, and
pay a shilling for four-penn'orth of liquor, and be
driven into a state of melancholy madness by the
sight of the misanthropic waiter? To the weekly
meeting of the Antediluvian Abnormal and Infantile Teetotal and Abstinence from Camomile-
tea Association? Or (and perhaps this is the
only reasonable amusement open to him, save
Miss Falsequaver's Grand Annual Evening Con-
cert at the Brummel Assembly Rooms, Mile
End, or Mrs. Indigo Hose's weekly literary and

scientific conversazione), shall you take your uncle on a rapid voyage of discovery from panorama to panorama, improving his knowledge of geography at every step, making him read as he runs, but slightly fatiguing, not to say boreing him, at last, with the endless unrolling of the Buried Cities of Eujaxria, the nine thousand and odd miles of the river Bödjudschka, the imperfect grammar of Mr. Sprottles the lecturer on Timbuctoo, and the villanous grumbling of the Harmonium at the Diorama (three miles long) of Mount Abora, including the Farnese Oberland and the Patagonian Chain. What more, I sternly ask, James (apart from the delectations of private society, late oyster-shops, Kamtschatkan Twins and Mysterious Ladies, which last three species of amusement none but a maniac would ever patronise),—what more than these can you offer to your respectable relation in this wonderful night-world of London? For his name is Plappington, not Cleofas; yours James, not Asmodeus. You cannot seize him by the cloak, and fly high

with him in air, unroofing houses as you go, a
supernatural Teddy the Untiler.

True, without being Asmodeus and a fiend, you
might show your uncle sights that are within
every man's ken and reach—sights that might
interest, and might instruct, but would afford
him, I opine, but scant amusement; more likely,
seriously affect the digestion of that good dinner,
and make him toss sleeplessly upon the Tavis-
tockian feather-bed. For an uncle to see such
sights his name should be Plato, not Plappington,
he should come from the groves of Academe—not
Cogglesbury; then might be found a nephew to
give him a rare night's roving; to show him the
sorrows and the shames, the stony-hearted horrors
of the streets, the dead secrets of the river, the
unutterable miseries of the hovels in the city that
is paved with pure gold. To stand by the hospital-
door where the sick go in—to stand at the hospital railings where the corpses come out—to
bathe oneself in the ruby glare from the cheap
doctor's shop—to listen to the never-ending clang

of the pawnbroker's box-doors (private boxes, and
the Inferno performed every night)—to hear the
oaths of the wan carpenter in the garret, when he
finds his tipsy wife has pawned his Sunday coat
—and the cries of the wan woman in the cellar
as the drunken cobbler beats her head in with
his lapstone—to see how the boys are thieves at
eight, and the girls lost at twelve, and all of them
ragged and starved at any age; and then, *presto*,
to hie away to new springs and pastures, to broad,
open squares and spacious streets, clean, well-
paved, and fresh-smelling, there to see the coro-
neted carriages roll, the proud horses champing
at great men's doors, the splendid footman hand-
ing up the foaming tankard or the fog-defying
drop of short to curly-wigged coachee on the box;
the comely housemaids darting out from number
three to fetch the beer, and hear the latest news
of ribbons, the Life Guards, and missusses from
number four; the visions of fragile forms of fair
women at drawing-room windows, and of shawled
and cloaked figures hastily entering or issuing

from carriages. These sights and sounds would suit Plato, but not your uncle Plappington. The philosopher would find matter for weeping and laughter, for cogitation and speculation; but your worthy avuncular hop-merchant would, in all probability, indignantly tell you, that he was not going to be dragged through the slums of the East-end and the genteel deserts of the West, and if you thought that the way to treat your father's brother, sir, you were very much mistaken.

It is my opinion (I do not hold it to be accurate, but as Montaigne says, it is mine) that the foregoing tableau is a tolerably faithful one of our much vaunted London Nights' Entertainments. I am not aware of the existence of any more remarkable amusements myself, and I have run the gauntlet of and become tired of them all.

But supposing now, dear reader of mine, that your name, instead of James, was Jules—that you were a student of medicine, say in the Rue St. Jacques, in Paris, deeply immersed in researches in osteology and the anatomy of the Closerie des Lilas. Supposing your uncle, M. Bonenfant, to be arrived in Paris from Picardy, where he is nursing for you (and uncles with something to leave to their nephews seem to be far more plentiful in France than in England) that snug little *propriété*, where there are so many poplar trees, and pigs as lank as grey-hounds, to say nothing of the comfortable amount of *rentes* standing against the name of Bonenfant on the Grand Livre. Supposing him to have given you a nice little dinner in the Rue Dau-phine—not too much wine, but enough, and of the very best : that you have had your *petit verre* and coffee, your evening paper and game of dominoes at the Café Belge afterwards; and supposing he were to say to you, "*Eh, bien!* Jules, my child, whither goest thou to take thy uncle this evening ?"—how facile would be your reply. Of course you would not suggest the before-mentioned Closerie des Lilas, the Prado, the Salle Montesquieu, the St. Cécille, Valentino, or Wauxhall. Your uncle does not play billiards, and the display of being addicted to such sports might render in future the good man somewhat chary in the remittance for " books " and *inscriptions*—the two unfailing items in the student's budget of ways and means. Still, your solution would be easy. As a Frenchman, naturally your first proposition would be to visit the spectacle, the play; but if you had dined late, or there were no good pieces in vogue just then, you would as naturally say, " My uncle, we will take a walk on the Boulevards." And by the Boulevards I mean, not only that limited space of asphalte pavement, gas-lamps and half English cafés, ordinarily patronised by my much-observing countrymen in their visits to Paris, but the whole line of busy, thronged, brilliant streets, that stretch unrivalled and unexampled for magnificence in Christendom, from the Madeleine to the Temple, the Boulevards des Italiens, des Capucines, Montmartre, St. Denis, St. Martin, du Temple, Beaumarchais, and de Strasbourg.

On that inimitable thoroughfare are enacted the far-famed Parisian Nights' Entertainments. They can be matched, equalled, rivalled, nowhere. They are subject to no cessation. On high days they are; on holidays they are; on days of fast and humiliation they would be, if Frenchmen ever fasted or humiliated themselves. They are entirely gratuitous. No saxpence here and sax-pence there repulse the pilgrim who would much like to be entertained, but has no money to pay for his entertainment. If you have money, so much the better: you may drink, smoke, buy sweetmeats, and be merry; but if you be smitten with the plague of impecuniosity, you may take your fill of the Parisian Nights without the expenditure of a sous. There is a toper's ditty, I have been told, called "Which is the properest day to drink?" The question is answered by other topers, who, after recapitulating all the days of the week, gravely decide that every day, from Monday to the Sunday following, is a drinkable day. If I be asked which is the properest time to see the Parisian Nights' Entertainments in their greatest perfection, I answer—all times; they are never out of season; and the winter entertainments vie with—but in no manner surpass—the summer ones. Let me, reversing the order of the seasons, take winter first, and follow my visionary Jules and his equally mythical uncle in their pursuit of amusement.

The old year has said his say, and fought his fight out. He has hung up his sword, and his helmet is a hive for bees. To-night is New Year's Eve, and the Boulevards, always a little crazy, even at the best of times, go stark staring mad. A myriad swarm of petty merchants—small industrials who vegetate during the rest of the year no man knows where—suddenly start up from their occult hiding-places, and furnished with the necessary permissions from the all-Paris-pervading police authorities of the Rue de Jerusalem, rush on to the Boulevards laden with planks, merchandise, and carpenters' tools, and proceed incontinently to convert the great highway of

European civilisation into a fair. Do you know that charming lyric which, with "Cheer, boys, cheer," and "The good time coming," used to be, in the hands of an accomplished musical lecturer, one of the most popular London Nights' Entertainments?—the cheerful ballad, commencing—

> " Hark to the clinking of hammers,
> Hark to the driving of nails—
> They're building a gibbet and scaffold
> In one of her Majesty's gaols."

Well, all night long, on New Year's Eve, on his Imperial Majesty's Boulevards, you may hearken to the clinking of hammers and the driving of nails, and witness the building of gibbets and scaffolds, but not for the lugubrious purpose mentioned in the quotation: the gibbets are erected for no more suspercollatory end than to hang toy-watches, sham gold chains, and embroidered braces over; the scaffolds are only built for the display of sweatmeats, toys, and small wares. But clinking and driving the hammers and the nails work fast and furious the winter night through. An Aldershot of wooden huts, a Houvault of hovels, rises almost instantaneously from the kerbstone. You wish to cross the road: *presto,* your passage is blocked up by an impromptu booth. You gaze meditatively upon one of the young Boulevard trees (those expiatory columns of byegone *émeutes*): quick it is surrounded by planks, and its branches peer curiously over squeaking Punches and india-rubber balls. Did you ever see a lady play on the fiddle, reader? There is certainly no impropriety in the employment. Saint Cecilia doubtless had a favourite Straduarius; yet there does seem to be something indefinable, bizarre, fantastic, out of place, in fair hands taking up the fiddle and the bow. But if a feminine violinist be a novelty, what would you say to a lady carpenter? Here are some hundreds of them, hammering, sawing, chopping away, with tremendous vigour and celerity. These eyes have seen the grandam of eighty polishing off a plank with a plane to a

nicety: they have seen a trim little damsel of
seventeen, with a coloured handkerchief tied
coquettishly round her head, busily fixing beams
and girders, while a great bearded, bloused man
sat majestically by, smoking his pipe, or if he
condescended to interfere in business matters at
all, unpacking dolls' houses, or dabbling with a
glue-pot. What labour will not French women
undertake? They follow the plough; they keep
books; they open box-doors; they take tickets at
railways; they drag luggage to the Custom-house;
they cut you your chops and biftecks at the
butchers'; they dance on the tight-rope and on
stilts; they buy old clothes; they keep shooting-
galleries; they enter lions' dens; they measure
you for boots; they shave you (yes, sir, this
stubbly chin has been reaped many a time and oft
by Mademoiselle Virginie—long may she be an
ornament to the Rue de la Monnaie); and here,
by Jupiter! they are putting up the booths where
their merchandise is to be exhibited on the Jour
de l'An. It is my firm impression that French-

women are capable of, and willing to undertake every imaginable kind of labour, save and except only making beds, polishing oak floors, cleaning boots, and nursing babies. Those humiliating employments they abandon to the other sex.

It is just eight o'clock, and Paris, having pretty generally finished dinner, has emptied itself upon the Boulevards. Two compact, closely wedged-in columns of humanity flow on, the brilliantly lighted shops on one side, the busy booths on the other. Paris has just done dinner, and is complacent, good-humoured, and eager for entertainment. There are, perhaps, yet some thousands of late diners and late sitters busy over their Clos Vougeot, their Sillery, or Romanée Conti in the grand restaurants of the Palais Royal; they will come on to the Boulevards by-and-bye, and swell the complacent throng. There are perhaps, too, some other thousands who have not dined at all; but they are on the Boulevards already, amicably jostling those whose gastric juices are functioning, as if they could aliment themselves

by sympathy, and dine by contact. Much misery
in this crowd, doubtless, much crime, much im-
morality; many men coveting their neighbours'
houses; many haggard, long-haired, dissipated
blouses, eager to espy dangling watch-guards,
prompt to purloin incautiously-displayed hand-
kerchiefs. Many moody tradesmen, doubtless,
knowing that they must commence the new year
by a sad visit to the tribunal of commerce, there
to depose their *bilan*—declare themselves bank-
rupt; many hope-deferred, heart-sick men and
women, who are walking on the Boulevards for
the last time, who know that every street at right
angles to the great highway will lead them to the
quays, whereby flows the silent Seine; much
envy, remorse, vain wishes, discontent in this
bustling throng—who can gainsay it? But this
is but the alloy to the golden happiness of New
Year's Eve; the great body smiles, laughs, squeezes
its partner's arm, buys toys and goodies for its
children, gives halfpence to beggars, remembers
its good dinner with a soft benevolent retrospect,

is thankful for New Year's Eve, and gaily antici-
patory of New Year's Day.

More booths! No part of the lines of the
Boulevards could be free of them if it would—
which, considering that it delights in them, is not
very probable. The lordly Boulevard des Italiens,
with its clubs and *cercles*, its restaurants for
princes, and cafés for kings, is as beset with New-
year's booths as the humble Boulevards du Temple
and Beaumarchais. To be sure, the merchandise
exposed for sale becomes somewhat flimsier in
character, and cheaper in price, as the Italian
Boulevards—the head-quarters of fashion, luxury
and the Anglo-French visitors—are left further
and further behind. Look on and marvel at the
chaos of fancy goods heaped about, a small portion
already arranged for sale, but by far the greater
bulk heaped in apparently inextricable confusion
upon the kerb and roadway, and in and about the
wood-work materials of the half-completed booths.
Sweetmeats of every imaginable size, colour, and
variety of design, and, if their vendors are to be

taken at their word, of every possible phase of flavour: pectoral lozenges, pastes, anti-consumptive wafers, and *racahout des Arabes; galette, gaufres*, macaroons, *flan*, and many other edibles of the ambiguous order of pastry, more or less indigestible, but all very appetising to the sense, and richly brown in colour; toys, whose name is legion—trumpets, drums, tin sabres, sabretasches, miniature cannon, shakoes, artillery wagons, brass eagles, model knapsacks, models of Sebastopol (in which the French, Russian, English, and Turkish soldiers have all been evidently cast in the same mould, but whose nationality is now clearly distinguished by vigorous dabs of green, blue, and red), together with the whole train of mimic military accoutrements and appliances of which young France is so desperately fond; railway trains at full speed (if the vast columns of smoke, symbolised by cotton wool, issuing from the funnels of the locomotives can be taken as a sign of *grande vitesse*); donkeys with panniers, accordions, woolley horses drawing bakers' carts,

fifes, tambourines, old gentlemen with gouty toes
and moveable mouths, musical snuff-boxes; dolls,
in the form of *cent-gardes*, *guides*, *pompiers*
with shining brass helmets, sappers and miners
with huge muff-caps and huger beards, and the
semper-florent tribe of languishing lady dolls of
all ages, with red shoes, long auburn ringlets,
bright blue sashes, stiff muslin skirts, and staring
eyes; pigs that squeak, curly poodle dogs that
bark, eels that wriggle, elastic babies of gutta-
percha painted black, birds that sing, wheel-
barrows, hares and tabors, spades, whips, camels,
rattles, corals, rocking-horses, percussion guns,
bronze pop-pistols, miniature kitchens, outfitting
warehouses (in these little model shops the
relative tastes of French and English are admirably displayed). In our London repositories a
very popular toy is the model of a butcher's shop,
with wooden legs of mutton and gaudily-painted
sheep. In France, the favourite model is that of
the establishment of a *marchande de modes* or a
magasin de nouveautés — money-boxes, marbles,

humming-tops, Punches and Pierrots. But not to toys or sweatmeats alone are the *étalages* of the New-year's booths confined. Here you have braces and garters tastefully worked, bead-purses, porte-monnaies, papier-mâché portfolios, work-baskets, belts, bird-cages, wafer-stamps, paper-knives, card-racks, fire-screens, looking-glasses, liqueur-stands, flower-pots, dressing-cases, and music-books. Nay, you shall not travel far before you see booths, where are positively offered for sale, sets of fire-screens and hardware, and chests of drawers, arm-chairs, and washhand-stands. Now, considering that the purpose for which this city of booths is notoriously erected is the purchase of New-year's presents, and more-over that the persons who make these *étrennes*, or New-year's gifts, generally deliver them to the recipients *de vive main*—by their own hands—a poker, tongs and shovel, or a neat marble-covered washhand-stand, would not, at the first blush, seem exactly the sort of article suitable for a present on New Years Day. Comfortable and

T 2

convenient would be those articles of furniture, doubtless, and exceedingly useful to young beginners not over-encumbered with household stuff; still, from their nature and conformation, too heavy and bulky to be easily conveyed under a gentleman's arm into a friend's house, or in a lady's reticule to the residence of a female relative.

This system of New-years' gifts giving, by the way, is the most terrible nuisance, annoyance, burden, infliction, tax, penance, and unutterable bore of all things French within my experience. You can't help yourself, for he who would refuse to give his *étrennes* on the *Jour de l'An* in France, is unworthy the name of a Frenchman or a Briton, as the case may be. Refuse to give *étrennes*, and you are a marked man, a being to be avoided, distrusted—a wretch to be suspected of exciting citizens to hatred and contempt of one another, and therefore amenable to the several social penalties that that mysterious offence can call for; a vagabond as irreclaimable as

Robert Macaire, as accursed as Kehama, as banned as the wandering Jew. The greatest social crime in England, after being in debt to your washerwoman, is to refuse a penny to a Guy Fawkes; in France, next to being in debt to your *concierge* for wood, postage, and messages, you cannot commit a graver offence against decorum than to be behind-hand in your New-year's presents. Such a recalcitrant is a bad subject, a man of *rien du tout,* of nothing at all, a *mauvais* droll, a bad droll, an *ours Martin,* a *cancre,* a *jobard,* an infinity of other names still more idiomatic, and still more untranslateable. Still, the infliction is awful. Frenchmen themselves grumble at it, inveigh against the practice with indignation frightful to behold, and passionate invective worthy of Mirabeau; but they are obliged to submit to it as one of the institutions of the country, as we to church-rates, a territorial aristocracy, county magistrates, and the Court of Chancery. The very Government seems to legalise the abominable custom; for on New

Year's Day it disseminates official promotions wholesale, and scatters crosses of the Legion of Honour broadcast. Now, supposing that you are resident in Paris, and mixing in decent Parisian society, and that you have an income of say 5000 livres, or £200 per annum. On New-year's morning, miserable morning, you have to trot the entire circle of your acquaintance, know-ing, Miserrimus, that you are growing poorer and poorer at every door you visit—leaving here an expensive *cornet* of bonbons, here some chocolate worth perhaps fifty sous in a gimcrack casket that cost, very probably, fifty francs; here a whole bandbox full of toys; here a host of nicknacks as useless as they are expensive. The higher the society you move in the more valuable your presents are expected to be. If you consort with countesses you must give away jewellery, forsooth, bracelets, brooches, and what not; very jocund and gay are the booths on the Boulevards this New Year's Eve; but, ah! how much bitterness and woe must there be in the sight of these gay trifles to him who has to give away presents to-morrow! Little can he enjoy the Parisian Nights' Entertainments.

THE CHILDREN'S HOSPITAL.

I should like to take some hard-handed, crusty-headed capitalist—a contractor, who, with a grim joy in the work, will run you up a penitentiary or an union workhouse in any given number of months—a pacer of the Exchange flags, and wearer-out of the stone stairs at Lloyds', a stern statist and political economist, with his head and his mouth full of disagreeable facts about " surplus population," " laws of supply and demand," " doctrine of averages," and the like—a callous, case-hardened, cynical man of the world, who, though he does not condescend to acknowledge it, holds but by three articles of faith : that poverty is crime, that success is virtue, and that the week-day Bible (there are some of the class

who will even throw you in the seventh day) is
the banker's book;—I should like to take a man
such as this—cold, case-hardened, frozen-up, inflexible, backing the Lord Mayor when he complains against the intolerable sin of alms-giving,
applauding country justices when they send
nursing mothers and destitute children to the
infamy and contamination of a jail, paying rates
and taxes, and grumbling consumedly at these
imposts, but gloomily repelling all solicitations
for charity, thinking the police-court poor-boxes a
dangerous innovation, soup-kitchens a mockery,
refugees for the destitute a delusion, and baths
and wash-houses a snare;—I should like—having
first caught my man of the world, after having
led him through many moving scenes of London
misery, after having heard him tell a blind man
that he ought to be ashamed of himself for
begging, and bid a cripple to go and work—to
cast him into a hansom cab, land him at a house
in Great Ormond Street, deliver him over to a
matron or comely nurse, and when he has spent

an hour in a certain mansion of pain, and when
I got him down in the entrance parlour again,
poke him suddenly in the midst of his white-
waistcoat, ask him what he thought of the establishment he had just visited, and boldly ask him
for a cheque or any loose sovereigns he had about
him. I am not by any means rich. The West
Indian estates don't yield anything like the sum
they were wont to do; and my transactions
relative to Telegram and Toxopholite are not of a
very promising description; yet I don't mind
betting very long odds that nine out of ten
callous worldlings, such as I have sketched, would
respond to my appeal, by offering me a pinch of
snuff, and forthwith bestowing a generous dona-
tion upon one of the most charitable and merciful
institutions in the metropolis, the Hospital for
Sick Children. Yes, I am glad, thank Heaven,
to be able to think well enough of my fellow men
to believe this. I will go further, and say that I
don't mind venturing a small additional bet, by
way of rider, that beneath the white waistcoat

there would be an unusual throbbing; that in the
voice so used to quoting prices-current and in-
sisting on hard-bargains, there would be an unac-
customed huskiness; that in the stony gray eyes
there would tremble a drop of unfamiliar brine.
For Trapbois was a child once, and Harpagon
must have played at ball, and John Elwes, the
miser, had once a little sister. As for the better
majority of men and women, as for those who
cherish loving memories of the dear innocents
who have been taken from them, who are haunted—
but in no fearful ghastly manner—by tiny ghosts,
it will need, I am sure, but increased knowledge
of an admirable and beneficent establishment to
secure the warmest sympathy, and the most
earnest support for an hospital, yet struggling, I
am sorry to say, against many difficulties, but
needing only the cheerful God-speed and helping
hand of the public, to extend the sphere of its
benevolent influence tenfold.

Though hospitals of the kind before us have
existed in the principal cities of the Continent,

from Paris to St. Petersburg—nay, even in Prague and Constantinople—for a considerable period, London was, until the last ten years, entirely destitute in this respect; and it was not till 1843 that the subject even began to be mooted, owing to the researches of the Statistical Society. The lamentable fact that, to quote the eloquent words of Mr. Charles Dickens, " of all the coffins that are made in London, more than one in every three is made for a little child—a child that has not yet two figures to its age," gradually took hold of the minds of some benevolent persons, and evoked their sympathies. At last a house was taken, and wards were opened; and the Hospital for Sick Children is now in the twelfth year of its age.

It was a grand old mansion in Great Ormond Street at whose portal three days since I struck a modest double-rap. A double-knock at the door of an hospital! And yet—I did not dislike the notion though, for it had an air of home in it —I could not help speculating, as I stood in the spacious entrance hall, at the foot of the wide staircase, with its carved bannisters, and waiting for the arrival of the nurse, who had been summoned by the courteous matron to show me over the hospital, upon the many vicissitudes the old and out-of-fashioned house had gone through. There were traces of rich carvings, mouldings, and other decorations about; some magnate of the Law or Senate lived here, doubtless, when Bedford Row was an aristocratic locality, and Lord Thurlow lived in Bloomsbury Square. Drums and routs, assemblies and "spadille, manille and basto parties" were once held here. Hoops and brocade have rustled and flustered down those stairs; the dulcet music of the harpsichord has been heard echoing through those spacious chambers; romping children have raced, loud-laughing, from floor to floor. There have been silvery voices and jolly songs heard here in the old time, and the house has been full of brave company. Now again it is as full as it can conveniently hold; but it is only full of little people

who suffer, who are very still and quiet, who
seldom—very seldom—laugh or play, and who
die sometimes. You might hear a pin drop in
the vast house. There is no romping, no pattering
feet, no silvery voices. Only now and then throbs
the velvet tread of the nurse carrying food and
medicine, the firmer but still gentler tread of the
house-surgeon; only now and then you hear a
feeble little wail, the laboured effort of impeded
respiration, the weary but not querulous sigh of
the bedridden cripple. For they suffer very
patiently and uncomplainingly, these poor mites,
the nurse tells me, and bear their tiny crosses
bravely; nay, in the intervals of pain they can be
cheerful and playful enough. They break down
when their friends come to see them, sometimes;
mother and father, and aunt, and sister who is
strong and hearty, are too much for them, and
for some time after the visit they fret and grizzle;
but they soon pick up again, these weaklings, and
become as happy as their infirmities will let them
in their other home, the hospital.

In the first ward I entered,—The Girls',—I saw seated in the centre of the room (that it was exquisitely clean, airy, comfortable, and well ordered, I need scarcely say; for, to their honour, the same may be repeated of all the hospitals built by that benevolent architect, "Mr. Voluntary Contributions"), huddled up in a tiny chair, a poor little crippled child. It was a case of "rickets," and it seemed hopeless. I shall never forget the inscrutable-pondering, anxious-inquiring look in the child's face. It was as though sickness was to her some big enigma, some monstrous conundrum, of which the solution is lost. By times a ray of weary pain would flash across the wan little face; as though the child had been indulging in a bright day-dream, had been dreaming that she was very strong and active, that she could jump, and skip and dance with the other children after school, and had then awakened to find herself there, in the midst of the clean-scrubbed room full of beds, bound down to a chair in the hopeless reality of the rickets.

Some wistful eyes followed us. A comely young nurse, who had somewhat of a melancholy expression, as though her first cousin the baker, or that wild young fellow the butcher, had been trifling with her affections, and had so led her to the soothing occupation in which I found her, led me round the Girls' Ward; but in very many cases, alas! the little sufferers 'let us go by with listless, mournful unnotice. One poor child, coiled up almost into a ball among the bed-clothes, could not bear the light—I forget the name of her disease—and was always shrouding herself thus; another, covered with dreadful cutaneous sores, lay stark and rigid out, as though waiting for death, and a merciful release from pain. I started, though, when the nurse told me that the child was getting better wonderfully, and that hers was a very hopeful case indeed. The children were all in iron-work cribs, lightly and commodiously made, and which possessed a capital contrivance in the shape of a sliding board on the top rails, which when the child was well enough to sit up in bed, and brought close up to its breast, formed an excellent play-table and platform for its toys. And its toys! I never felt so much disposed to acknowledge what benefit Messrs. Farley and Merry, and their brother toy-merchants, are to society.

The mantelpieces of the hospital—Boys' and Girls' wards—were covered, the cupboard was full, the tables and beds were sprinkled with toys. None of your penny monkeys that run up sticks; none of your scarlet spotted horses, whose heads come off at the first tug at the bridle; none of your hideous "Catch 'em alive, O" monstrosities; but sound honest toys. Livery stables, my dear madam, with spirited proprietors in wooden boots, gleaming with black, and wooden faces radiant with red shininess; dolls to be danced with string, donkeys with panniers, brewers' drays, butchers' shops, boxes of bricks, sets of tea-things, sets of furniture, and regiments of grenadiers. On one of the mantelpieces there was a monumental Noah's Ark, a triumph of naval and zoological impossibilities. How I should like to be First Convalescent and a good girl, for to her is doubtless granted the privilege of disentombing the animals in the ark, of lugging up the elephant through the roof (with Shem wedged between his fore-legs), and extricating the zebra from his unpleasant entanglement between the camel-leopard's hoofs and the donkey's hind feet. I saw no painful toys, and I am glad of it. I don't like those squeaking, grunting, gasping figments, that you have to pinch or squeeze before you can get any fun out of them. Above the children's heads, and on the walls at their sides, hung simple coloured prints; there was the infant Samuel on his knees, and the good Samaritan raising up the man who went down to Jericho and fell among thieves; there was little Eli and his mother; and there was a picture of the Temple, where He sat among his disciples and bade them suffer little children to come unto Him. As we passed from bed to bed, we came every now and then to a young invalid sitting up, and gravely playing with his toys. In one corner, a child and two others who were up and dressed and convalescent, I suppose, were cuddling over that meritorious institution a picture book, and seemed to derive much solemn delight from its contents. The gentlefolks, the nurse said, brought the toys; but not only the gentlefolks, the poor brought them, the doctors brought them. I am growing a confirmed gamester, for I will wager that on his second visit to the Hospital for Sick Children that cynical friend of mine in the white waistcoat would bring toys enough with him to stock one of the shops in the Chain Pier at Brighton. There is a loving, thoughtful kindness in thus ministering to the wants, the weaknesses, the innocent pleasures of these infantile patients, that cannot be too highly commended in the patrons and directors of the hospital. The very out-patients' receiving ward, where so many as two hundred children are sometimes received in one day, is hung round with pictorial cartoons of a popular nature—birds, beasts, and fishes, history scenes, Bible scenes, views of famous cities. Such representations are adverse to the doctrines of political economy, I am aware; but who shall tell but they will now and then help to assuage a little pain, and make minutes of agony the shorter?

There were fifteen girls in this ward, the ages ranging from three to ten. There was a case of typhoid fever, another of croup, a very sad one of rheumatism, but the most painful was a "starvation" case. The child had been received a few days previously, in almost a dying state, from inanition and neglect; due, it is but just to say, more to the extreme and hideous poverty than to the cruelty of its parents. The face was like a diminutive death's-head. The nurse drew up one sleeve of the child's bedgown, and showed me a bone; yes, a bone just covered with integuments. "Lor,' sir," she said, in answer to an expression of horror, "it's getting quite plump to what it was a week ago."

The arrangements in the Boys' ward were

similar to those that I had already seen. There was the same scrupulous cleanliness, the same tidiness and air of general comfort, that pervaded the Girls'. The boys were more lively, though; two or three, who were convalescent, were clinging to the nurses' skirts. More were sitting up in bed, and one was playing in a most animated manner with a kitten. All who were able to do so greeted us as we passed, with a little airy wave of the hand, that was full of genuine courtesy. Little children are little gentlemen.

Bath rooms with sitz and shower baths, a large and airy garden for those children sufficiently recovered to take exercise, a *perambulator*, and a medical theatre in course of construction, these were among the things I glanced at during a hasty visit, and all bore testimony to the judicious and forbearing kindness which actuates all concerned in the management of the hospital. I may add too, and am glad to have such a duty to perform—that the nurses seemed full of gentleness and tenderness towards their infant charges,

and there were not wanting some unmistakeable
indices on the part of the children themselves,
to show how lovingly grateful they were for the
care and trouble bestowed on them. It was
evident that "Mrs. Sairey Gamp," and "Mrs.
Betsy Prig," that the rampant, drunken, ferocious,
rapacious school of "Sawbones" nurses, had no
abiding place here—but, psha! who *could* be
hard with these lambs?

I came out of the hospital very humiliated and
womanish, and yet proud of the pious zeal, though
I possess it not, which has established and supported this refuge for suffering childhood. And
I was consoled somewhat, when I thought, that
we have all, the very humblest of us, the means
of furthering a good work, if we only use our
best endeavours. I have done my best here
to place before you something like a notion of
the interior aspect of an institution, than which
I am certain there is not one in this vast metropolis worthier of support and encouragement.

ENGLISH MILORDS.

THE writer of this piece once upon a time, and in a foreign land, suffering from an attack of the megrims, or *diaboli cærulei*, sought solace and delectation in a place of public entertainment situated on the Boulevard Montmartre, in Paris, called the Salle Bonne-Nouvelle. Here, for the consideration of one franc, he was gratified by the view of a series of *poses plastiques;* of a remarkably stupid ballet, in which a floury-faced Pierrot went through the ordinary tribulations incidental to Pierrots when brought into collision with comic fathers, jealous millers, and village maidens in short petticoats; but all of which did not in the least remind him of the only supportable Pierrot in the tumbling world : the inimitable

Deburcau. He was furthermore entertained by a mysterious round or catch, sung by three persons in three white waistcoats and one pair and a half of kid gloves, which, together with the remaining pair and a half of hands, would have been none the worse for a little washing, and in which a large tuning fork supported a considerable part; by a "Juggler of the Alps," than whom the author has seen many better; and, finally, by a gentleman attired in a short green coat, labelled, conspicuously, " *Patente* " (*sic*), a pair of widely checked trousers, also labelled " *Patente*," with the addition of the royal arms of Great Britain beneath the label; highlows and gaiters, a white hat with a narrow brim and a black hat-band, a huge shirt-collar, a gigantic umbrella, red hair, green spectacles, a very diminutive carpet bag and a long pig-tail, each and all branded with the omnipresent " *Patente;* " who, as an obliging neighbour of the writer informed him, was made up to represent a *Milord Anglais*, and looked the character

—as that neighbour further volunteered to tell him—remarkably well.

This British nobleman sang a song to the old tune of Malbrook, accompanied by some feeble gesticulations imitative but not suggestive of the noble art of self-defence. The writer, on his affirmation, declares that, as nearly as he can recollect, the first verse of the English peer's song ran thus:—

Malbrook s'en va-ti li BOXE
L'ami de Pitt et Fox
Aow yes! Aow yes!

Each couplet being interpolated with an Aow yes! and each stanza being concluded by a facetious and profoundly ironical allusion to one "Matinkosh," probably synonymous or connected with that waterproof garment so useful in travelling, or to the gentleman whose place of residence was so strongly and inflexibly negatived on his personal application some years since. The Milord's song was encored amidst the most enthusiastic demonstrations of approval and delight; but the writer, being momentarily diverted from the stage and orchestra by a supplementary entertainment, or *pièce de circonstance,* not in the bill of the evening—consisting in the scampering of three mice through the pit, and the heroic efforts of the *sapeur-pompier* on duty to capture and immolate them with his sabre—did not enjoy the repetition of a ditty so flattering to his national pride, and soon afterwards left the Salle Bonne-Nouvelle, and walked home.

Now I, who am the writer, as I walked through the snow, thought of a certain Emperor, who, like the man who won an elephant at a raffle, won four hundred thousand armed men in a *coup,* and didn't know what to do with them; of the Peace Congress; of the militia, our naval defences, the Minié rifle, the conical bullet, screw steamers and the Digue at Cherbourg; also, of the stupendous amount of international ignorance existing in the two greatest countries in the world—of how little the English know about the character and customs of the French, of how much less the French know about those of the English.

The origin of the English Milord, as brought under French consideration, is either lost in the mists of obscurity, or is beyond my ken. But the English Milord was looked upon in France as a species of drunken savage, frequently cutting other people's throats, and not unfrequently going raving mad, tyrannising over his dependents, and mercilessly beating his wife and children, until about the middle of the reign of Louis Quatorze, the *grand monarque.* In those days the restoration of Charles the Second taking place, and the exemplary Count Anthony Hamilton, and others of his class being a good deal backwards and forwards from Paris to London, the French nobility condescended to discover and admit that their brother peers in England could be every whit as heartless, as politely depraved, as fashionably blasphemous, as genteelly corrupted, as urbanely insulting, as wittily insolent, as " honourably " dishonest, as they were themselves. Thenceforth, and for a time, the Milord looked up. The offensive nickname was temporarily withdrawn, and he became the "*Seigneur—the Grand Seigneur Anglais.*" Molière condescended to nod to him. La Fontaine patronised him. Boileau would dedicate his next ode to him. But one Milord Cavendish who threw an insolent *petit-maître* on to the spikes of the orchestra of the Opera House brought the Milord into ill odour again. After the revolution, after the numerous Jacobite conspiracies of King William's time, after the first Scotch rebellion, when the Continent teemed with disaffected Scotch and Irish noblemen and officers—the Milord became once more a gryphon, a bogie, a hideous fable.

Voltaire, who ought to have known England and the English well, is rather shy on the subject of the English Milord. He shirks him. He treats of him a little in his Siècle de Louis XV., concerning the battle of Fontenoy; he tells you elsewhere that the Milord is one of that bizarre country where they "cut off the tails of horses and the heads of kings;" but, on the whole, he is reserved and taciturn on the subject of the

English Milord. *He knew him* and the ridiculously false impression entertained of him by the French; but he did not, doubtless, consider it worth his while to undeceive them just then.

Rousseau hated English Milords as he hated most people who strove to do him good (which many English noblemen and gentlemen essayed to do). There is spleen against the English nation and aristocracy scattered through his writings ; but the philosophic citizen and " philanthropist " of Geneva, knew too well what England and the English were, systematically to abuse or vilify them. Yet he upset no fallacy, exposed no error. In the *Nouvelle Héloïse* he has even gone out of the way to misrepresent the Milord: who assumes the guise of a morosely pensive misanthrope, skulking about cataracts and mentally browsing in deserted grottoes.

So continued the English Milord to the time of that old novelist of Louis Seize's time, Pigault le Brun, the only palliation of whose indelicacy

lies in his always making virtue to prevail and
vice to be chastised at the end of volume III.
Pigault le Bruu's Milord was an austere yet
ruffianly, proud yet jocose, avaricious yet muni-
ficent, accomplished yet coarse-spoken aristocrat
—a sort of *mélange* of Squire Western, Sir
Charles Grandison, Pigault's own Monsieur Botte,
Voltaire's Doctor Pangloss, and our English
Commodore Trunnion. He travelled about in a
postchaise, fitted up half as a tavern, half as a
doctor's shop, always with a beautiful daughter,
always with a negro page whom he beat and
kicked and gave unnumbered guineas to. He
swore tremendous oaths at postilions. He was
the terror of postmasters, cooks, scullions, inn-
keepers and chambermaids. Lastly, he had an
irresistible *penchant* for adopting orphan children
(boys), and ultimately marrying them to the
charming Miss, his daughter and sole heiress.

Pigault le Brun lived far into the Empire; but
the time and scene of his novels are mostly laid
at a period anterior to the Great Revolution. In

the days of the Republic, the Directory, and the
Consulate, the Milord Anglais assumed quite a
new phase of character. He became, all at once,
an emissary of "*Pitt et Coburg*," always hovering
about the frontier of France, or mingling in disguise among its population; went about laden
with sacks of English gold wherewith to bribe
the enemies of freedom. The English Milord
kept head against the *bleus* in the impenetrable
bocages of the Vendée; his gold it was that kept
the army of Condé organised, who nerved the
conspirators of the infernal machine to their
desperate attempt, who brought Georges Cadoudal and his murderous Chouans to Paris.
The contagious breath of English Milords (headed
by that arch Milord, Nelson,) blew the flat-
bottomed boats of Boulogne to the winds, and
caused that *regrettable sinistre*, Trafalgar.

When the fatal obtuseness of the Milord Wellington, who never could discover when he was
beaten, had brought (treason aiding) the allied
armies to Paris, the English Milord, chameleon-

like, once more changed his hue. Then was he
first heard of as a boxer, as an eater of raw beefsteaks, as a maker of tremendous *paris* or bets,
and as a monomaniacal amateur in horseflesh.
The English being just then the strongest, and
being through their upholding of the house of
Bourbon on good terms with the French aristocracy, there was in Paris, from 1815 to 1818, a
species of Anglomania or Milordophobia in which
the Milord Anglais was the *arbiter elegantiarum*,
the "cynosure of all eyes," "the glass of fashion
and the mould of form.' Novelists, dramatists,
essayists, artists immediately seized on the new
English Milord and made a lion of him. He
was represented in the salons of Frascati and the
gambling rooms of the Palais Royal, wrenching
handfuls of sovereigns from the pockets of his
great-coat with many capes, and throwing them
wildly on the *rouge* and the *noir*. He had horses
in his drawing room and "bouledogues" in his bed.
He boxed continually. He drove vehicles like
cockle shells (or like those rendered so famous by

Mr. Romeo Coates and Mr. Pea Green Haynes),
he dined sumptuously at Véry's and Vefour's,
and he drank (which is perhaps the only thing of
the series that the English Milord did really and
truly do, during the occupation of Paris by the
allies) enormous quantities of execrable champagne, which he thought delicious. That
champagne plot was the greatest, sweetest, most
ample revenge the French. ever took upon us for
Waterloo; and the disgrace of that day has been,
to my mind, completely washed out by the floods
of bad champagne which were foraged out from
the cellars of Rheims in 1815, bought by specu-
lators at about seventy-five centimes a bottle, and
sold to the English and the Cossacks at about
from six to ten francs. Was not *that* vengeance
on the Islanders and the Barbarians?

The English Milord once more changed during
the latter part of the reign of Louis XVIII., and
the whole of that of Charles X. There was a
famous piece called *Les Anglaises pour rire*, performed at the Palais Royal, in which not only

Milords but Miladis were ridiculed, and which had an astonishing run. After this the Censure, the gloom-inspiring domination of the Jesuits, and the novels of the Vicomte d'Arlincourt, with perhaps, some ugly shreds of news from England about Luddites, and spies, and Thistlewood with his head off, made the English Milord quite a different character. He became a stiffnecked, morose, gloomy *Grand Seigneur* terribly affected with a mysterious malady called *le spleen* (there is a three-volume novel about one Sir Williams, afflicted with that ailment), travelling austerely about Europe with a sulky suite, and two four-gons full of sauces and French cooks. According to M. de Balzac (when he was M. de Viellerglé) —who was so fond of depicting English Milords, that he occasionally wrote himself under the pseudonym of one Lord R'hoone (!)—the Milord Anglais lived hermetically sealed up in a frowning hotel with high walls, a mulatto porter, fierce wolfdogs, and one little garden door of egress, from whence he was supposed to issue to accom-

plish all sorts of dark and dreadful deeds.
According to M. Casimir Delavigne, and M.
Alexandre Dumas in the early days of their
dramaturgical career, the Milord had no longer
beautiful daughters, but always one son, Sir
Arthur, a villain, continuously breaking promises
of marriage to confiding French females, and
throwing his helpless offspring on the hands of
his papa, who at first would have nothing to say
to them, and cursed them, his son and daughter-
in-law, with all the forms; but, ultimately relent-
ing, endowed them with his enormous estates,
and the insignia of the order of the Bath. The
Milord Anglais of that day had strange fancies
for ascending Mount Vesuvius during eruptions,
holding grim champagne and "Porto" orgies in
the catacombs of Rome, poisoning his servants,
shooting brigands, and writing letters in his own
blood. Horrible nobleman!

The tragic Milord disappeared after the revolution of July '30, to give place to an eccentric one.
There was a semi-serious one about 1843, who

was supposed to have made an enormous bet that Mr. Van Amburg would one day be devoured alive by his wild animals, and always followed him about from country to country, and from theatre to theatre, always occupying the stage box, and fixing on him the foci of an enormous opera glass. This Milord had green eyes! In Louis Philippe's time, however, eccentricity became, as I have said, the distinguishing character of the English Milord. He dressed—in the press, on the stage, and on canvas—in a bell-crowned white hat, a long loose white great-coat, red striped small-clothes, top boots, a mighty shawl swathed round his flaming countenance, a plaid waistcoat, an umbrella, and a pigtail of course. One or more savage " bouledogues " always lurked at his heels. His course of life might be summed up with considerable facility, so regular was it. He rose at ten, breakfasted off raw beefsteaks and *vin de Porto,* playing with his bouledogues and smoking a pipe meanwhile. At eleven he had the spleen. From half-past eleven to twelve he

betted with his coachman; from twelve to one he
boxed with his groom. From one to two he
drank gin or "grogs." At half-past two he sold
his wife, Miss Kitty, in Smithfield with a halter
round her neck. From three to four he drove
tandem in Cheapside — four horses at length.
From four to five he had another refresher of
beefsteaks with "porter beer." From five till
midnight he bet, drank, smoked, and boxed with
other lords, and after an indefinite number of pipes,
bets, and grogs, fell *ivre mort* against an *honorable*
barronet, membre de la chambre des lords, and was
carried up to bed by his groom, or tiger—Joby,
Toby, or Paddy. If I have exaggerated one trait
in the character of the English Milord, tell, oh
ye authors of *Les Mystères de Londres, Le Marché*
de Londres, Les Voleurs de Londres, and *Clarisse*
Harlowe. Towards the end of the reign of Louis
Philippe, the Milord Anglais varied the course of
his diary by occasionally oppressing Ireland, and
sucking the life-blood from the slaves of Hindo-
stan. It also occurred to him to turn perfidious;

" French commerce to destroy and reserve to
himself the empire of the seas." The Milord
was then and for some time known as a " Pritch-
ard," but the salient parts of his character remained the same.

After the Revolution of February and the exchange of visits between English excursionists
and French National Guards, one more, and as
far as it has gone, ultimate change took place in
the counterfeit presentment of the Milord Anglais.   He became purely but extravagantly
ridiculous, wearing the egregious costume, and
speaking the barbarous balderdash, of the Salle
Bonne-Nouvelle.   As such he flourishes at all
the theatres, and in all the *feuilletons* of Paris; at
Valentino, in caricatures, and in the *Journal pour
rire*, and as such is taken for granted, though
there are hundreds of well-dressed Englishmen
walking daily about the Boulevards and the Rue
de Rivoli, offering a fair field for caricature, and
not in the least like him.

Now what ever, I ask, can have propagated,

nourished, perpetuated for nearly a hundred
years this monstrous ignorance of what Englishmen are like, of what they do, of how they act,
of what are their manners and customs? Heaven
knows we have prejudices enough to get rid of,
and mistakes enough to correct in our own country concerning foreigners; yet, ignorant as we
are, I think were an actor, representing the part
of a Frenchman, to appear in an English theatre
wearing a pigtail and a cocked hat, eating frogs,
and accompanying the operation with a solo on
a dancing-master's kit, the calumniator would be
hooted or pelted from the stage. With an eleven
hours' route from London to Paris, with railways
and a submarine telegraph, with myriads of
Frenchmen in our streets, the French seem
really to know less of us every day. Balzac said
that there were only three Frenchmen in France
who could speak French: Victor Hugo, Théophile
Gautier, and himself. It might almost be said
without exaggeration that there are only three
people in France who know England and the

English: to wit, M. Léon Faucher, M. Guizot, and that certain Personage before alluded to in connexion with the elephant in the raffle.

There may perchance be found some little excuse for the ridiculously false notion the French have formed of our habits, institutions, and literature, our good and bad points, in the eccentricities of a certain class of travellers who infest foreign seaports, railways, and hotels, who are the bane and nuisance and standing scoff thereof. Why don't they stay at home? They go back to their own country more ignorant (if possible) than when they started. They grumble at dinner, insult landlords and waiters, pertinaciously cling together to avoid learning the language of the country they are in, and then abuse and vilify each other, and moan and fret because they can't speak it. They carry with them their grievances and prejudices, and sectarian hatreds and prejudices, their ladies' maids (confound them!) and their physic bottles. They are good friends and honest people, but the worst travelling companions in the world. It is not through any private or personal griefs that I pass these strictures on the conduct of some of my countrymen travelling abroad; but it is, because I think that if a certain section of them were to stay at home, or, when they travel, were to think what the great ends of travelling should be—improvement, observation, and sensible recreation, with a reasonable deference to peculiarities, a little subservience to custom, a little less ill-temper, and a little more docility and willingness to learn—the Milord Anglais would be somewhat more fairly drawn.

CAVIAR AND RUDESHEIMER.

A SHILLING book of Thackeray's
   I lately bought at Aix-la-Chapelle,
And read it as I travell'd north,
   A-munching of a Rhenish apple :
[Not that I really ate the fruit ;—
   'Twas merely said to turn a rhyme, a
Task I am now intent upon,
   O'er Caviar and Rudesheimer.]

The famous dish of *Bouillabaisse*
   [As vile a mess as e'er I tasted]
The mighty Makepeace he hath sung—
   A *critique* on it would be wasted.
But as I set the lines to tune,
   And with my foot beat softly time, a
Thought came across me that *I'd* sing
   Of Caviar and Rudesheimer.

Now, Caviar's dried sturgeon's roe

   [A fish that haunts the deep so vasty]—

Some think its flavour exquisite,

   And some intolerably nasty.

'Tis glossy, granulated, black,

   And cover'd with a salty rime, a

Device to raise the thirst you slake

   With copious draughts of Rudesheimer.

There are some little cakes of bread

   [Not thicker much than vermicelli] ;

On these you spread the Caviar,

   Which looks like salt black-currant jelly—

Or rather jam ; and then you crunch

   One tempting morsel at a time—a,

And take to each half-dozen bits

   Say, half a flask of Rudesheimer.

Twice three long days I've journeyed on,

   Along the northern German road—a;

The day is damp—the chimney smokes—
    And I'm at Stettin-on-the-Oder.
Remote, unfriended, sick and sore,
    I know not how to pass the time—a;
I cannot read the "*Fremdenblatt,*"
    And so I fly to Rudesheimer.

There! let the stupid world go slide:
    'Mid chickens, donkeys kick their heels up;
See! here the smooth-shaved *kellner* comes;
    Again my ruby glass he fills up.
What's Love? a sigh; what's Life? a lie;
    Is truth on tap in any clime—a?
The *summum bonum* here below,
    Is Caviar and Rudesheimer.

The King of Prussia drinks champagne;
    Old Porson drank whate'er was handy;
Maginn drank gin; Judge Blackstone, port,
    And many famous wits drink brandy.

Stern William Romer drinketh beer,

   And so does Tennyson the rhymer;

But I'll renounce all liquors for

   My Caviar and Rudesheimer.

If Prussian thalers I'd per ann.

   One thousand [just three pound a-week 'tis],

I'd scorn the golden treadmill's round,

   And cry to conquerors " *Væ victis !* "

My blue-eyed Gretchen she should spin,

   And I would loaf away the time—a,

And smoke and sing the live-long day,

   With Caviar and Rudesheimer.

I'd have my rooms three storeys high,

   With balconies the street o'erhanging,

Whence I could see the children play,

   And hear the quack his gulls haranguing.

But, ah ! I've not a pound a year;

   Nay, oft for weeks I've not a dime—a.

And so I dare not even dream
    Of Caviar and Rudesheimer.

If some kind heart that beats for me,
    This troubled head could e'er be press'd on;
If, in the awful night, this hand,
    Outstretch'd, a form I loved could rest on;
If wife, or child, or friend, or dog,
    I call'd my own, in any clime—a,
This lyre I'd tune to other strains
    Than Caviar and Rudesheimer.

Stay! there's a poodle, who's my friend,
    Shaved "Henri," far across the ocean:
But, bah! I'm maudlin; t'other flask
    Will chase this babyish emotion.
Her hair was light, her eyes were bright;
    I heard her bridal—death-bell, chime—a;
Here, *kellner!* take away the glass;—
    My eyes are dim with—Rudesheimer.

Inspector Symons is an ass—
   He may be right, though, in his praxis;
What, though the moon does not rotate
   And hasn't even got an axis?
The earth is square—the sky's pea-green—
   'Tis half a mile from Hull to Lima;
And I'm as drunk as any lord
   On Caviar and Rudesheimer.

THE END.

www.ingramcontent.com/pod-product-compliance
Lightning Source LLC
Chambersburg PA
CBHW060524030726
47498CB00004B/1064